AN ASSASSIN PREPARES

By N. J. McIver

AN ASSASSIN PREPARES
COME BACK, ALICE SMYTHEREENE

AN ASSASSIN PREPARES

N. J. McIVER

PUBLISHED FOR THE CRIME CLUB BY

Doubleday

NEW YORK

1988

All of the characters in this book
are fictitious, and any resemblance
to actual persons, living or dead,
is purely coincidental.

Library of Congress Cataloging-in-Publication Data

McIver, N. J.
An assassin prepares.

I. Title.
PS3563.C373A87   1988   813'.54   87-33070

OG

AN ASSASSIN PREPARES

The week before I contracted to kill John "The Baron" Barany the Museum of Modern Art ran a series of movies the general theme of which was murder for hire. *Hollywood Hit Men, 1940–1980*, and very timely it was. I saw six of them in four days, a sort of crash course in how to be an assassin.

They were all there. Charles Bronson, Lee Marvin. Richard Widmark pushing the old lady down the stairs in her wheelchair. Jack Palance blasting the silly little sodbuster in the muddy street in front of the saloon.

My favorite was Alan Ladd. *This Gun for Hire.* Tough and impassive, with that pretty-boy face hinting at some core of softness behind the emotionless eyes and deep, taut voice. I liked that film so much I even got the book out of the library. *Murder didn't mean much to Raven* is how it begins. *It was just a new job. You had to be careful.*

"Murder doesn't mean much," I told my reflection in the bathroom mirror. "You just have to be careful."

I dropped my voice half an octave below its normal range and tried to make my eyes opaque, which wasn't easy. I had to squint, having misplaced one of my contacts the day before. After a while I gave up looking in the mirror and concentrated on the voice.

"Carry a book," Jerry told me over the phone. "Something she can recognize you by."

"This Gun for Hire," I said without hesitation.

"A how-to-do-it book, huh?" was his response. "I guess they have them on everything nowadays."

I wasn't sure if he was joking.

"I already talked to her about it," he continued. "She'll be carrying something called *Madame Ovary.* Paperback edition."

"Uh, are you sure that's not *Madame Bovary?"*

"Ovary, Bovary, whatever. I don't think there'll be too many people carrying books up there on a nice summer day, do you?"

"Uh, that reminds me, Jerry. Don't you think that Riverside Drive is a little too, er, public? I mean shouldn't we be meeting in the back booth of some Eighth Avenue bar or something like that?"

"Of course it's public. That's the idea. You meet each other in broad daylight for a look-see, a little chat. Then if you both go for the proposition you meet later in a hotel room to make the contract. That's how it's done."

What did he mean, "that's how it's done"? What did he know about it? I was the one who had been seeing all the movies.

"Besides, who's going to be looking at you? You could stab each other to death and nobody would do anything about it except turn the volume up on their Walkmans."

"Well, I know, but I just thought . . ."

"You're not paid to think. Just act. Leave the thinking to me."

A born director, Jerry.

He was wrong about nobody carrying books. I

counted over a dozen during the half hour I spent next day waiting for my client to arrive. A veritable book fair was Riverside Drive that warm July morning, with reading matter that ranged from *Ayatollah's Love Slave* to *Teaching Your Cat to Program in BASIC*. But no *Madame Bovary*. Or *Madame Ovary*, for that matter.

On the other hand, Jerry was right about no one noticing. The drive was full of people, the usual mid-morning crowd. Mothers and babies, joggers and lovers, scholars and hustlers. On the bench next to me a pair of old men in undershirts were playing cards. Across the street a vagrant lay sleeping at the base of an equestrian statue, his cheek nestled against a pint bottle with brown paper bag for pillowcase. And there in that vortex of city life I was as alone and unnoticed as a hermit in the desert.

Well, almost. There was an old lady, not more than four-feet-ten in heels, who kept walking her Pekinese back and forth in front of my bench. From the way she eyed me each time she passed, I could have sworn she was trying to pick me up. She wore a faded sundress with stockings rolled down to her ankles, displaying a pair of spindly, milk-white legs so richly embossed with purple splotches of varicose veins they might have been painted by Jackson Pollock. I stared at the legs as she passed, being something of a fan of abstract expressionism, and she must have caught me at it, for she stopped and gave me a coy smile. I buried my face in my book.

Raven picked up the automatic again. Who could have imagined an old lady could be so tough?

"Is that book any good?"

She had sat down next to me on the bench. The Peke was sniffing at my shin.

"Huh? Oh, all right."

"Any good sex scenes?"

"Uh, no, I don't think so."

"This one's loaded with them."

She reached into a pink plastic beach bag sitting on the ground between her legs. If it's *Madame Bovary*, I thought, I'm bugging out.

She held up a worn copy of *Hollywood Wives.*

"Some real hot stuff."

A cab had pulled to a stop on the other side of the drive, and a woman stood next to it paying the driver. I peered myopically at her to see if she fitted Jerry's description, but all I could tell at that distance was that she had long blonde hair. The rest was a blur. As soon as the cab pulled away she straightened up and, after a few quick glances up and down the row of benches on my side, started across the street with long, determined strides. By the time she was half-way across I could see that she was tall and sun-burned, wearing a lime-green, summery kind of dress and carrying a large straw shoulder bag and a paper-back book.

"You want a piece of fruit?"

My benchmate was leaning toward me, extending a plum-laden hand. I decided on a small change of scene.

"No thanks. I have to go meet someone."

I rose from the bench and took a step in the direction of the approaching figure, but the Pekinese had sniffed a complete circle around my right leg, and the leash snapped taut as I stepped forward, sending me sprawling onto the pavement. *This Gun for Hire* slipped from my grasp and skidded down the street, ending at the base of a tree about eight feet from where I lay.

The blonde stopped in her tracks and looked warily around, first at the crone on the bench, then at me on the sidewalk. The Peke ran back and forth across my back, digging his claws in and yapping excitedly. The end of the leash had fallen out of the old lady's hand and wrapped around the beach bag, dragging it forward and leaving a trail of three plums, two peaches, a heel of pumpernickel, a *Daily News*, eight rolls of pennies, a ball of wool, a pair of knitting needles, a half-eaten prune Danish, a bottle of suntan lotion, and a copy of Playgirl.

I saw the blonde stiffen, then turn as if to walk away.

"I see you are an admirer of Flaubert," I called after her. They were code words, of course, the opening sentence of a little piece of dialogue with which to identify ourselves. You've seen that sort of thing in spy movies, I'm sure. I had made this bit up myself two days earlier, though at the time I had envisioned the two of us seated side by side on a bench, looking straight ahead and speaking *sotto voce* with very little lip movement, rather than me shouting from the sidewalk, lying in a pile of fruit and whatnot, with my back being torn to shreds by a Pekinese.

She stopped, turned back, and looked at me.

"I see you are an admirer of Flaubert," I repeated, speaking slower and louder and pointing as discreetly as possible under the circumstances to where my book lay under the tree.

She walked over to it, picked it up and examined it thoughtfully. I tried to smile reassuringly as I extricated my leg from the leash. By the time I got to my feet she had reached a decision.

"Not especially, but I do feel great empathy with Madame Bovary," she said as she handed me the book.

"A woman in trouble is always a figure of sympathy," I responded, according to plan.

"You're telling me," muttered the old lady from behind me. Glancing over my shoulder I saw that she had recaptured her dog and was staring at us with a mixture of curiosity and hostility as she repacked her beach bag.

"Unless she can find a man who is willing to help her," said the blonde, thus completing the preliminaries.

"You're late," I growled through my teeth.

"Yes, I know. I'm sorry, but I had trouble getting a cab."

She looked me up and down.

"You sure don't look anything like I expected. Not that I ever met a hit man before, but . . ."

"Why the hell don't you speak up a little louder," I whispered angrily. "There may be a few people over on West End Avenue who didn't hear you."

I threw nervous glances in all directions. No one seemed to be paying us any attention. The old lady was absorbed in wiping a bruised peach with the hem of her sundress.

"Let's get out of here." I grabbed the blonde by the wrist and steered her toward a stone staircase that led down to the park.

"You don't seem very, er, professional, you know," she panted as I hurried her down the stairs.

She was right, of course. I don't usually go up like

that. In fact, I rather pride myself on my ability to stay calm and keep my concentration in the face of disaster. Like the time at the Wichita Shakespeare Festival when Juliet fell off the balcony and I improvised a six-minute monologue while the understudy got ready and the stage crew rigged up a stretcher. Without ever dropping character, I might add, and in damned near perfect iambic pentameter.

Well, once a trouper always a trouper. I pulled the blonde across the path at the bottom of the steps, through a small clump of trees into a little clearing, where we were alone.

"Okay," I told her, "let's keep calm and get down to business. Did you bring the money?"

"I think this has been a mistake," she replied, rubbing her wrist. "Maybe we should just call the whole thing off."

I was prepared to deal with a little hesitation.

"Suit yourself, lady. It was you who came looking for me."

I gave her a withering look of scorn, remembering not to squint.

"Maybe I'm just a little nervous," she said. "After all, I've never done anything like this before."

I shrugged to show her it was everyday business to me.

"I'm just not sure what to do. It seems so, well, final and all."

I gave her a level stare. *Murder doesn't mean much to Raven*, I tried to convey with my look. *It's just a new job.*

"Could I think it over?" she asked. "Maybe get in touch with you some time next week?"

I sneered.

"In my business you don't get two chances. By next week I might be in Palermo."

I watched her closely while she thought it over. Even without my contacts I was aware of the vivid greenness of her eyes. They were beautiful eyes. In fact, everything about her was beautiful, from the long blonde hair to the shapely stockingless legs. She was a knockout, just the type I have always been a sucker for, and I would have fallen in love with her on the spot if she hadn't been hiring me to kill some other guy.

"All right," she said finally, looking straight at me, her eyes narrowing slightly as she spoke. "Let's go through with it."

"You sure?"

She nodded once, then looked away.

"Okay, then." I tried to sound businesslike. "Did you bring the money?"

"No, of course not. You didn't expect me to just carry four thousand dollars around with me, did you?"

"Well, how soon can you get it?"

"A few hours." She looked at her watch. "Say about three o'clock?"

"Okay. Three o'clock, then. You come to the Hotel Clayton on Forty-eighth Street just east of Seventh Avenue. I'll be in room 311."

"Are you kidding?" She shook her head. "Not on your life. If you think I'm walking into a strange room in some sleazy midtown hotel, you're crazy. You come to my place."

Jerry hadn't said anything about going to her place. My instructions were to get her to the Hotel Clayton.

"It's a perfectly respectable hotel," I told her. "I stayed there on my senior class trip to New York."

She shook her head again, but less forcefully.

"Arlene Francis used to do a show from their coffee shop," I lied. It did the trick.

"Oh, what the hell," she said. "I guess one place is as good as another."

"Three o'clock, then. Hotel Clayton, room 311. You want to write that down?"

"No, I'll remember. Forty-eighth Street, right?"

"Just east of Seventh. Knock three times, then pause, then knock two more."

She smiled broadly. Her teeth were gorgeous.

"Kind of like a spy movie, huh?"

"It's just a job," I said. "You have to be careful."

"Sure."

"Bring the money in small bills."

"Okay."

"Tens and twenties."

"Fine."

"I'll need some photographs of the, er, subject."

"The subject? Oh, you mean John. I have them with me, as a matter of fact."

"Well, bring them to the hotel. Close-ups?"

"Three close-ups, all from different angles, plus one full-figure shot."

"I guess that's it, then. You take off now. I'll see you at three."

She looked so pretty as she stood there nodding solemnly, her green eyes wide with excitement and fear, I wanted to put my arms around her and hold her tight against me. But I watched her turn and walk quickly back the way we had come.

"Hey!" I called after her. She stopped and turned

around. "What do you really think of *Madame Bovary?*"

"What?" She seemed surprised by the question. "Oh. I never read it. I mean, I just started it."

"Oh."

"I saw the movie."

"Jennifer Jones and Joseph Cotten?"

"Yes."

"Well, what did you think of that?"

She reflected a moment.

"I thought she was kind of a jerk."

With that she turned and walked away. As soon as she was out of sight I sank to the grass, dropped *This Gun for Hire* beside me, and stared, exhausted, at the sky. No role had tired me so much since the dancing banana in the Fruit Chews commercial.

After a little while I became aware of movement, something rubbing against the bottom of my trousers. A sniffing noise came from the vicinity of my shoes. I reached into the breast pocket of my jacket for my glasses, put them on, and sat up. The Pekinese was running his nose along the soles of my loafers.

"Oh my God!" I cried.

"I heard you," said my friend from the bench, not bothering to offer me a piece of fruit. "I heard you talking to that girl. I know what you do for a living."

Raven would have killed her on the spot. I just scowled.

"Listen." Her voice dropped to a hoarse whisper. "How much is it?"

"Huh?"

"What do you charge? You know, for your services."

"Er, you must have misinterpreted our conversation," I said, scrambling to my feet.

"It's my husband. I can't stand him no more."

As I reached down to retrieve *This Gun for Hire* the Peke began circling my legs.

"Okay, I knew he wasn't much when I married him. I admit it. I was desperate to get away from my mother and I figured he'd grow on me. But forty years of boredom is enough."

"I'm sorry, lady. I'm already engaged."

I took a step away from her and tripped on the leash.

"It doesn't have to be today."

"I'm booked solid for the next six months."

I tried to untangle myself, but the Peke kept snapping at my hand. She pushed him away and leaned toward me.

"He's such a slob, you'd be doing the world a favor. And there's a lot of insurance. Maybe we could collect double indemnity, like in the movie with Barbara Stanwyck and what's-his-name."

"Fred MacMurray. He got caught."

I swiped at the Peke with *This Gun for Hire* and missed, but managed to wriggle free of the leash.

"What kind of businessman are you?" she shouted after me as I ran full speed toward the staircase. "Things are so good you can afford to run away from a customer?"

So ended my first morning as a professional assassin.

2

Let me explain how I became a hit man.

It started last October when my car plunged ninety feet off the bridge that links Maple Valley with Pine Ridge. You know the one I mean. I'm sure you've seen it dozens of times. I had been drinking and it was raining, but the real cause of the accident was Dr. Todd Duncan's tampering with my brakes after he learned I was having an affair with his wife.

Naturally, the fall killed me. I didn't take it lying down.

"What do you mean they're writing me off the show?" I asked Morrie Ritz. "I've only been on it for three months."

"Length of the contract, kiddo. They're not picking it up."

Morrie is my agent. He calls me kiddo. He calls everybody kiddo. I've been with him two years and I don't think he knows my name.

"But why?" I demanded. "Everyone said I added a lot to the show. The director liked my work. I even have a following. You know how many fan letters I got this month?"

Morrie shook his round, bald coconut of a head.

"Not the point, kiddo. They need a murder trial. Haven't had one in over six months. And the producer wants Dr. Todd Duncan to be the accused, thinks he'll win a lotta hearts in the witness box. Which leaves you holding the bag as the victim."

He leaned across his desk and grinned at me, dropping his voice to a conspiratorial whisper.

"Besides, Lisa Duncan is gonna turn lesbian. I got it from one of the writers. After your death she has a nervous breakdown, gets sent to a sanitarium and falls for the head nurse. But, if it's any consolation to you, she's gonna have your child some time in January."

"Boy or girl?"

Any irony in my tone was lost on Morrie.

"What's the difference? The poor kid's gonna be raised by a couple of dykes."

Strange as it may sound, I drew no comfort from the news that a fictitious child of mine was going to be born to a neurotic lesbian on a soap opera. Besides, I was sure it wouldn't even live to see its first birthday. The average life span of a newborn on that show is about three months. So much for "A Brighter Tomorrow."

"Anyway, kiddo," said Morrie, fingering his bow tie, "you're better off without that *chazerai*. You're an artist."

"Well, it's nice of you to say that, Morrie, but even Edmund Kean had to eat once in a while. Can't you get me a commercial?"

He looked skeptical.

"The last one I sent you out on, you fainted."

"Well for crying out loud, I was zipped up tight in twenty pounds of banana costume, wasn't I? I nearly died of asphyxiation."

"All right, all right. I'll do what I can. Give me a call in a couple of weeks."

He flashed me a smile he must have copied from a used-car salesman.

"Of course, if you need something in a hurry, there's always Hot Harold. One of the Hunks pulled a groin muscle."

Morrie Ritz is not one of New York's top agents. One indication of that is the location of his office, half a block west of Ninth Avenue. Another is that the only one of his clients that works regularly is a group of male strippers known as Hot Harold and the Hunks. For two years, on and off, Morrie has been offering me work as a Hunk replacement.

"You can join 'em in Scranton tomorrow and I guarantee you three months on tour. At five hundred a week and all you can . . . heh, heh."

He winked. I sighed.

"No thanks, Morrie. I'll tough it out here in New York. Maybe I can get something with Shakespeare in the Park this summer."

"Whatever you say, kiddo. *Chacun à son gout.*"

He pronounced it 'gowt,' like the disease of the joints. *Chakoon a soan gowt.* Each to his own disease of the joints. It suited my mood.

"Did he offer you a job with Hot Harold again?" asked Teresa as I passed the reception desk.

I nodded glumly.

"And you turned it down, naturally."

I nodded again.

"Good!" she said emphatically. "Not that I don't think you're a hunk, Elliot." She rolled her eyes and grinned. "But you've got too much talent for that crap. Just hang in there. Your day will come."

"Thanks, Teresa."

"You were great in that thing about the whale."

"Thanks, Teresa."

Teresa Gianelli is Morrie Ritz's secretary and receptionist. Also his bookkeeper, file clerk, coffee maker, and sandwich fetcher. Not only does she know my name, she even came all the way up to Connecticut to see me play a harpooner in *Call Me Ishmael*, the off-off-off-Broadway musical version of *Moby Dick*. You may not have heard of it. It closed the second night.

"Hey, Elliot, you doing anything Saturday night? My brother Rocco has a couple of tickets to the stock-car races. I'll even give you dinner first. I make a mean lasagna."

"Uh, gee, that's very nice of you, Teresa, but I'm afraid I can't."

Teresa is actually rather attractive. Tawny skin, jet-black hair, dazzling teeth, and soulful brown eyes, all packaged in a solid if slightly over-lasagna-fed frame. But I had two reasons for turning down her invitation, just as I had turned down several previous offers. The first is that she has a lot of older brothers. I'm not sure exactly how many, but enough to outfit a small aircraft carrier, all with names like Rocco and Vito and Angelo, and jobs as stevedores and truck drivers and union officials, and I have this neurotic fear that their chief form of recreation is beating up guys who take out their sisters without marrying them. The second reason I couldn't go out with Teresa is that I was spoken for.

"You still going out with that snooty brunette who did the Perm-a-Lilt commercial?" asked Teresa.

"Oh, you mean Maud?"

"Yeah. Maud." She made the name sound like a species of fungus.

"Actually, we've been living together for the last two months."

"Oh," she said glumly. "I didn't know that." Then she brightened a bit. "Well, nothing lasts forever."

Quite a prophet, our Teresa. A regular Cassandra. Nothing lasts forever. Six months after she said it my unemployment insurance ran out. One month later Maud followed suit.

She broke it to me over a late breakfast one Sunday.

"Elliot," she began, innocently enough, "don't you think you ought to be looking for work?"

I smiled at her over the Arts and Leisure section of the *Times*.

"Actually, I'm reading for Joe Papp tomorrow. And Morrie says . . ."

"No, I mean work. You know, a job."

For the next half-minute I choked helplessly on a bit of croissant.

"You mean a *job* job?"

"Yes."

"Like in an office? Or waiting on tables?"

"Well, you don't expect to live on Perm-a-Lilt residuals forever, do you?"

We sat in uncomfortable silence for a minute or so. She poured another cup of coffee and sipped it slowly while I tried to fathom her reason for setting in motion such a terrible train of thought. Then, without looking at me, she said quietly, "I have a new job myself, by the way. In California."

"In California? For how long?"

"I don't know. Maybe forever. I'm going to be Binky Bannerman's assistant."

"Binky Bannerman?"

"You know. The host of 'Getting and Spending.' We watched it last week when you were getting over the flu, remember? It comes on right after 'Leave It to Beaver.' "

"You mean that show where a bunch of lobotomy cases try to win refrigerators by guessing celebrities' weights?"

"That's not all they have to do. They have to answer some hard questions first."

"And Binky Bannerman is the guy with the alabaster teeth who keeps shouting 'It's time to get and spend'?"

"I don't know anything about his dental work," she answered coldly.

"And you're going to be his assistant? What does that mean? You wear a bikini and read the numbers off the scales?"

"It's a big opportunity for me."

She made it sound like a Guggenheim Fellowship.

"Maud, I hate California. It's full of game-show hosts and all kinds of other things I'm allergic to."

She didn't answer.

"Maud, I don't want to go to California."

She took another sip of coffee, then put down the cup and looked me straight in the eye.

"Elliot, I don't know how to tell you this exactly, but nobody invited you."

I mentally allowed as how she had just done a pretty good job of telling me exactly, but I limited my for-the-record reply to a simple "Oh."

As I helped her pack during the next few days, I reflected on the prospect of life after Maud and decided I was not all that sorry to see her go. Nine months of living together had somewhat dulled my appetite for Maud, whereas it had not at all dulled her appetite for Chinese food, eaten in bed while listening to recorded music of a rather cloying type. Nothing against Mu Shu pork, mind you, but it does put a fellow off his stride to land in a puddle of duck sauce when cuddling up to his mate.

Untidy though she may have been, however, Maud did have redeeming virtues. Solvency, for instance. She had always paid her share of the rent. And for the last few months she had paid mine as well. She would be leaving a gap that would not be easy for me to fill, what with having been killed in a horrible car crash and subsequently exhausting my unemployment insurance. I brought it up one evening while packing her collection of Barry Manilow records into a cardboard carton, taking the cheerful and reasonable tone with which one friend invites another to join in a constructive round of mutual problem solving.

"Oh, you don't have to worry about meeting the rent," she assured me. "I've sublet the apartment. Would you hand me the Englebert Humperdinks on the next shelf?"

"You've what? How could you do that? How could you sublet our apartment without consulting me?"

"*My* apartment, Elliot. Remember? That was our agreement when you moved in here. Anyway, there's no point in discussing it. We have to be out by the end of the week."

"The end of the week? What are you talking about? Where the hell am I going to live?"

"Oh, you'll find something. Now be a dear and get the pictures down from the bedroom wall, okay? I think they'll fill out the rest of this carton."

The pictures on the bedroom wall consisted of eight photographs of Maud. I glared at them as I shouted into the next room.

"The least you could have done was offer me a chance to sublet."

"How was I to know you wanted to?" she called back airily. "You should have asked me sooner. Besides, I don't think you can afford it."

For a little while after she left—about eight hours, I think it was—I managed to live off my savings. Then, for a few more months, off a loan from my father. That was not without its price.

"Excuse me, sir," he told me via long distance from Cranston, Rhode Island. "You must have the wrong party. My name is Feinstein. F-e-i-n-s-t-e-i-n. Morton Feinstein."

"Dad, my name is Feinstein too."

"Pardon me, then. My mistake. I thought I was talking to a Mr. Elliot Fenway."

"Dad, we've been through this a hundred times. Fenway is my professional name, my stage name. In my heart I'm Feinstein."

"Ah."

My father has a real way with a monosyllable. He can make an "ah" sound like a Bellini aria.

"Ah," he repeated. "Now I understand."

He paused. Fortunately, I had called collect.

"Feinstein is the name in your heart, also good for loan applications. But for the credits that go before the public it's Fenway."

"Dad," I pleaded. "I'm desperate."

"And besides, who names themselves after a base-ball park?"

"Dad, we're New Englanders, aren't we? Red Sox fans."

"A Red Sox fan I've been all my life, but I never expected to be the father of the stadium."

At this point in the ritual we always observe a half-minute of heavy silence.

"Elliot," he finally said, "you're my son. I'll send you the money. But I gotta tell you I'm not going to be around forever. You're over thirty now and getting nowhere fast. Don't you think it's time you came home and settled down? I could use some help in the business."

"Dad, I can't. I'm sorry, but I'm an actor. It's my life."

He sighed.

"Okay, Elliot. We're both too old to argue. Who should I make the check out to?"

"Uh, it would probably be a little more convenient if you made it out to Elliot Fenway."

"Okey-dokey, Fenway it is. Listen, give my regards to Elliot Feinstein if you happen to run into him."

The one bright spot in the whole sorry picture was the offer of a rent-free apartment for six months from my friend Phil Bender. Phil and I were roommates back in the days when we were both newcomers to New York, and since then he has made a sizeable fortune designing computer graphics for TV commercials.

"Just take care of the utilities," he said in response to my insincere offer to pay part of the rent. "I'll handle the rent. It's worth it to have someone occupying the place. And it saves me the expense of putting a lot of things in storage."

Phil has been burglarized twice and is understandably nervous. He has even taken to keeping a small gun in the top drawer of the little commode in his living room.

"Though I still think you ought to come out to the coast with me."

Like Maud, Phil was defecting to Los Angeles, in his case to do the special effects for a series of sci-fi epics.

"I'll talk to the director. I'm sure he can find something for you. Maybe you could be the voice of the black hole."

"No thanks, Phil. I appreciate the offer, but somebody has to keep the country from tipping into the Pacific. Besides, I think I have a real shot at Shakespeare in the Park this summer."

Brave words. Little did I know as I said them that the only acting I would do in a park that summer would be my own adaptation of *This Gun for Hire* with a Pekinese as co-star. Down in Central Park, meanwhile, they managed to cast *All's Well That Ends Well* without me.

As I watched my bank account dwindle over the next two months, I wondered if I had made a mistake in not going west with Phil. Pickings were slim in New York that season, and I was about as much in demand as a pediatrician in Sun City. With very little money left, no jobs on the horizon, and no way I could in all decency put the touch on my father again —at least not successfully—there seemed no recourse but to go back to waiting on tables.

I had just taken my sturdy black shoes out of the

closet and polished them to a shine when I got a call from an old friend with an offer of work. An acting job, something out of the ordinary.

No, not another dancing banana. Much seedier.

3

"Take a contract for murder? Are you crazy? I'm an actor, not a gangster."

"Keep your voice down, for crying out loud."

Jerry De Marco glanced nervously around the dimly lit room. We were in the back booth of a dingy little cocktail lounge just off Columbus Circle, and the only other patrons at that early afternoon hour were a couple of middle-aged men watching a golf match on the TV and a hard-looking, red-haired woman of indeterminate age who sat mumbling to herself in a slurred voice. None of them seemed particularly interested in our conversation.

I am not in the habit of patronizing such places in the middle of the day. But Jerry, who arranged the meeting, is a nightclub comic with an aversion to daylight matched only by Count Dracula. His wife Gloria swears that he does not spend the sunlit hours closed up in a coffin. His jokes just sound that way.

"I know you're an actor," he resumed, after assuring himself that the gents at the bar were giving their full attention to Nancy Lopez. "An out-of-work actor, if you want to get technical about it."

"I don't."

"Okay, then I won't mention it. The point is I'm offering you a job, an acting job. You're not going to take a contract for murder, only *pretend* to take a con-

tract for murder. It's a *part*. Just like Mercurochrome,
only it pays better."

"Mercurochrome?"

"That thing you did down on Avenue B."

"Mercutio."

"Gesundheit."

Jerry's education in the classics of dramatic litera-
ture stopped somewhere around "Laverne and Shir-
ley." It is sometimes hard for me to remember that he
and Gloria and I once took acting classes together. In
those days I was sweet on Gloria and imagined a future of playing Hume Cronyn to her Jessica Tandy, a
dream from which I was rudely awakened by her
whispering in my ear during a classroom performance of Antony's death scene that she was three
months pregnant with Jerry's child. After that,
things were not quite the same between us. We
drifted apart and I lost track of them for a number of
years until they showed up one night at an evening of
Shakespeare a few of us had put together for the en-
noblement of the Lower East Side. What they call a
showcase, the kind of thing actors do for no pay in
order to be seen. I have spent more time in showcases
than a rhinestone tiara, but there is always the hope
of being picked out and worn to the ball.

"My point is," Jerry persisted, "that just because
you act in Shakespeare doesn't mean you really go
around saying 'forsooth' and 'methinks' all the time."

"I don't quite see what that's got to do with the
issue at hand."

"Well, just because you play the part of a hit man
doesn't mean you really do anything illegal."

"Not do anything illegal? Jerry, you're not talking
about some part on the stage. If I understand you

right—and I really hope I don't—what you are suggesting is that I swindle some woman out of a couple of thousand dollars by convincing her I'm a professional—"

"Elliot! Could you please keep your voice down? And don't say 'swindle.' "

"What do you want me to say? Con? Bilk? Okay, you want me to bilk some woman . . ."

"Elliot, please!" He glanced over at the bar. The redhead had started singing to herself. *Killing me softly with his song.*

"Listen." Jerry lowered his voice and leaned across the table. "She wants to have somebody killed. You take the money and don't do the job, you'll be saving some guy's life. You'll be a hero, except it won't get in the paper. Like an undercover cop."

"And I'll just happen to reward myself for heroism by pocketing a few thousand bucks of someone else's money."

"That's what I said. Like an undercover cop."

I shook my head.

"I don't have the nerves for it."

"What nerves? Who needs nerves? All you have to do is meet some dumb broad, make like Charles Bronson for a half-hour and collect an advance. What could be easier?"

"And what happens when I don't do the job and she realizes she's been had?"

Jerry shrugged.

"Let her report you to the Better Business Bureau."

"She's more likely to report me to the police."

"And tell them what? That she put out a contract

for murder? Think about it. There's nothing she can do."

He took a long swallow of Piel's beer, eyeing me over the rim of the glass as he drank.

"Besides," he said after licking his lips, "she won't even know who you are or where to find you."

"What if she recognizes me from the show?"

"What show?"

" 'A Brighter Tomorrow.' "

Jerry snorted.

"Are you serious? That was a year ago and you were only on it a couple of months. And not even every day. Your own mother wouldn't recognize you from that show."

"My mother never watches 'A Brighter Tomorrow.' It conflicts with 'All Our Yesterdays.' "

"Five hundred bucks, Elliot. For one performance. The easiest money you ever made."

"Five hundred bucks? Is that all? It doesn't sound like a lot of money to me. Not for what's involved."

"It's a lot better than Equity scale."

He became absorbed with a small stain on the cuff of his powder-blue silk shirt.

"How much am I supposed to collect from this woman?" I asked.

"You think this spot will come out?" He scratched it with his thumbnail. "I paid a hundred bucks for this shirt."

"How much am I supposed to collect?"

"I haven't worked that out, yet," he replied, examining his sleeve for further blemishes.

"Give me a rough idea."

He mumbled something indistinct in which I thought I caught the word "three."

"Three thousand?"

"Something like that. Three or four."

"Three or four thousand?"

"Yeah, maybe four. I think we agreed on that. But like I said, I haven't worked it all out yet."

"Four thousand!" I sputtered. "You're trying to hook me into some scam that nets four thousand dollars, and I walk away with five hundred? After doing all the work and taking all the risks?"

He raised his hands defensively, his face the picture of innocent helplessness.

"There are a lot of expenses."

"Like what?"

"Well, I have to rent a hotel room, for one thing."

"Oh yeah? Where's the hotel? St. Tropez?"

He looked hurt.

"Besides," he said, "I'm the one who's taking the risk. I have to deal with her afterwards."

I cut him off with a wave of my hand.

"That's not the point," I said frostily, sliding out of the booth. "Anyway, it really isn't a question of the money. The whole thing is just too degrading. I'm an actor, not some two-bit con man."

"How about seven-fifty?"

I stood up and glared down at him.

"You've done some low things in your time, Jerry, but this beats them all. I'm insulted that you would even approach me with such a sordid proposition. I may be going through hard times right now, but I haven't sunk that low."

"Seven fifty's the highest I can go."

I took a deep breath and squared my shoulders.

"I already told you it isn't a question of money," I said haughtily. "I am a serious person, an artist who has too much respect for his craft to lend it to such a disreputable scheme. You, on the other hand, seem to regard me as some sort of cheap bunko artist. That being the case, I think it's time we parted company. Thanks for the beer."

He looked up at me.

"Maybe I could make it a thousand."

I slid back into the booth.

"Tell me about it once more."

"There's not much to tell. I was out in Brooklyn a couple of nights ago to see some guy about doing a gig. I'm breaking in some new material, and I wanted to try it out in some out-of-the-way place, you know?"

As far as I knew, Jerry had not worked in any out-of-the-way or in-the-way place in over a year, but I withheld comment.

"I got a whole new routine," he said. "Did you hear about the guy with five peckers?"

"No."

"He has a wonderful tailor. Makes him pants that fit like a glove."

I laughed. I couldn't help it. Jerry did not crack a smile.

"Anyway, like I said, I went out to this nightclub in Brooklyn, told a few jokes, and the next thing I know, this broad starts coming on to me. You know how it is with some women. They can't resist a celebrity."

"It's never been a big problem with me."

"Huh? Oh no, I guess not. Well, anyway, I decided to have some fun with her, so I did a whole routine about life in show business. The places I've been, the stars I've appeared with, that kind of thing. And I guess I must have laid it on pretty thick about my mob connections. Some women really groove on that Mafia stuff."

"What mob connections?"

He waved the question away.

"Nothing. I made it up as I went along."

I wasn't so sure. Jerry and Gloria lived very comfortably in an Upper West Side apartment. A little too comfortably, it seemed to me, for their apparent means. Gloria had long ago given up acting for a job in a bank, and Jerry, as far as I could see, had given up working altogether. Not that he wasn't always full of plans—some unnamed benefactor having promised him a big booking in Atlantic City at some unspecified future date—but plans don't pay the rent, and I sometimes wondered what other sources of income Jerry might have.

"So," he continued, "there I am in the middle of my shtick, and she stops me and asks if I can put her in touch with a hit man."

"Just like that?"

"Just like that."

"So you decided to set her up with a fake one."

"I figured it was my duty as a citizen."

"I suppose I should be flattered," I said. "You need an actor to help you pull off a low, crummy swindle, and the first one you think of is me."

"To tell you the truth, the first one I thought of was Robert De Niro, but I figured he'd be too hard to get."

We sat in silence for a minute or so while I mulled it over.

"Count me out, Jerry," I said finally. "I just don't have the stomach for it. It's too far out of my line."

He gazed at me thoughtfully.

"All right, Elliot," he replied. I won't try to talk you into it. I understand how you feel." His face darkened. "I wouldn't get involved in it myself if I didn't need the money for Gloria's operation."

"Operation? What operation?"

"Nothing. Forget I mentioned it. I promised Gloria I wouldn't say anything about it."

"Jerry, don't pull that shit on me. I've known you too long."

"Forget it, Elliot. I shouldn't have said anything."

His voice cracked just a bit, and his eyes actually moistened. It was a four-star performance.

"It just gets hard sometimes, keeping it in."

He buried his face in his hands.

"Oh for God's sake," I muttered.

The truth was I was a little worried about Gloria. The last few times we had been together I had sensed a certain malaise about her, a despondency that even little Gary—he whose prenatal squirmings I had felt eight years earlier when, as the dying Antony, I lay on the floor of a Soho loft with my head pressed against the swollen tummy of Cleopatra—even he could not lift her out of.

"I don't believe a word you're saying," I told Jerry emphatically. "But if I really thought there was anything wrong with Gloria I'd be the first to help. You know that."

"Don't give it another thought, old friend. We'll get by."

"If this scheme wasn't so damned dangerous . . ."

"What's dangerous? You meet some dizzy broad in a hotel room for half an hour and put on an act. And for that you walk away with a thousand bucks. How many tables you have to wait on for that kind of dough?"

I thought of how swollen and sore my feet had been the last time I worked at Beefsteak Charlie's.

"What if she shows up with a couple of plain-clothesmen?"

"Oh for crying out loud, who do you think we're dealing with? Cagney and Lacey?"

"And another thing, I don't think a thousand dollars is fair. I wouldn't touch it for less than two. Fifty-fifty."

"Fifteen hundred."

I shook my head.

"Tax free," he pointed out.

"Forget it," I told him.

It was time to go. I was tired of sitting in that place. I slid out of the booth, stood up, and looked around. The redhead was no longer alone. Her head was resting on the shoulder of an overweight man in a plaid sports jacket. At the other end of the bar the middle-aged men were gone, their place taken by a pair of young couples engaged in animated conversation punctuated by raucous laughter. Above their heads the TV droned on unattended. The golf match had given way to some sort of game show, complacent voices of good cheer and grainy images of earthly delights radiating into the gloom.

"All right, fifty-fifty," said Jerry, grabbing my wrist. He looked up at me, his face troubled. "I guess I can find some way to break it to Gloria."

"I guess you can," I answered.

"*It's time to get and spend!*" boomed the TV happily. I looked up quickly. There on the screen, in a six-hundred-dollar suit, stood Binky Bannerman, beaming a toothy smile at all of us out there in America. And next to him in a one-piece bathing suit, as luscious as a melon in July, stood my ex-roomie Maud.

It made my heart ache.

4

Which explains how I came to find myself at two o'clock on a hot July afternoon in a seedy hotel room on West Forty-eighth Street waiting for the *knock-knock-knock*, pause *knock-knock* that would signal the opening of scene two of my life as a hired gun. Or was it *knock-knock*, pause *knock-knock-knock?*

For a film noir effect Jerry could not have chosen better than room 311 of the Hotel Clayton. The room looked as if nothing in it had been changed since the 1940s, including the sheets. Its lone window was streaked with grime and looked out across the sunless airshaft onto a tan brick wall punctuated by rows of dirty windows of its own.

I stood at the window in shirt-sleeves and suspenders—the last a nice touch, I thought. I had chosen a powder-blue shirt with thin, dark stripes, white collar and cuffs, and complemented it with a maroon necktie in which I had tied an immense Windsor knot. A shoulder holster might have rounded off the effect nicely, but I was afraid of overdoing it. Besides, I didn't know where to get one cheap and they aren't as comfortable to wear as they look in the movies, particularly in hot weather. Two years before I had worn one for seven nights running in a summer stock production of *Guys and Dolls*, and developed a nasty rash.

The jacket of Phil Bender's gray Palm Beach suit lay neatly folded at the foot of the swayback bed, and next to it sat the attaché case I had brought along for carting away the money. Inside the case was the tool of my new trade—Phil's .22 caliber pistol. Unloaded, of course. I did not want to accidentally shoot anyone, least of all myself. But props are important, and I had read in a detective story that those little .22 caliber jobs are favored by the pros. So, shoulder holster or not, I was going to give her a glance at the gun to let her know she wasn't dealing with an amateur.

She was late, a full fifteen minutes, and it was making me nervous. My shirt was sticky with perspiration. The temperature in the room must have been pushing ninety, and the window air conditioner, which looked like original equipment, wheezed and sputtered even worse than the cadaverous old desk clerk who had licked his lips and winked while handing me the key.

Finally there came a soft tap-tapping at the door. Before answering it I went and got the pistol from its case.

"Who's there?" I whispered fiercely.

"It's me. Roxanne."

"Roxanne?"

"You know. From Riverside Park. This morning."

Holding the pistol muzzle up, my forearm stiff, my elbow tucked against my ribs in the best Hollywood gangster tradition, I opened the door about two inches.

"Hi." She smiled nervously at me through the opening. I squinted back warily.

"You're late," I said through clenched teeth.

"I had trouble getting a cab," she replied.

"That's what you told me this morning."

"Well, the taxi situation hasn't improved since then."

"Also, you didn't use the signal."

"Look, do I get to come in or do we transact our business through a crack in the door?"

I undid the chain lock and opened the door. She entered, looking around with distaste and wrinkling her nose.

There was plenty to wrinkle at: the stale smell of the room, sweat of a thousand bodies laced with disinfectant and a heavy dose of thickly scented air freshener; the worn, lustreless look of the furnishings —carpet, bedspread, the upholstery on the lone, rickety chair, all were the same color. A dull, tired ochre.

"Boy, it's hot in here," she said.

"Did you bring the money?" I asked.

She did not answer, just glided silently to the center of the room where she stood looking cool as a Daiquiri in her lime-green dress, with her tawny skin and long limbs and soft yellow hair. She looked as much at home in those surroundings as a vase of gladiolas in a men's room.

"You live here?" Her tone made it clear what she thought of anyone who did.

"I do business here from time to time," I answered. "Did you bring the money?"

"Yes. Is that a real gun?"

"What do you mean, is it a real gun? What do you think it is?"

I realized I was still holding it pointed upward, so I lowered my arm and slipped it into my waistband.

"I just meant that it looks awfully small," she said. "For, er, professional use, that is."

We obviously did not read the same detective stories.

"The bigger they are, the harder they fall," I replied with a sneer.

"What's that mean?"

She had me there.

"Forget it," I said.

"You sure don't look like my idea of a hit man."

"Let's not use that expression, if you don't mind."

"Well, that's what you are, isn't it?"

"I prefer to think of it in other terms."

"Like what?" she asked.

"Like assassin," I said.

"What's the difference? It's the same thing, isn't it?"

Not by a long shot, but I didn't bother to spell it out for her. A hit man is some guy in a pin stripe suit with padded shoulders who guns down mobsters in restaurants in Little Italy. An assassin lurks in narrow alleys in renaissance Venice, wearing a doublet and carrying a poignard. Whatever they are.

"Forget it," I said for the second time.

"Well, call it whatever you want, you just don't look like one."

"Oh?" I snickered derisively. "And what does one look like?"

"I don't know exactly, it's just that you look . . ."

She scrutinized me carefully as she hunted for the *mot juste*. Then she smiled.

"Kind of cute, I guess."

Kind of cute! There I was in a seedy hotel room, packing a gun and preparing to take a contract for murder, and I had just been told I looked kind of cute. I glowered at her.

"Also," she went on heedlessly, "you look a little nearsighted to be a hit . . . er, assassin."

Enough was enough.

"I didn't come here to make small talk, lady. Let's cut the crap and get down to business. Where's the money?"

Her smile vanished.

"I have it right here. You don't have to snap at me."

She had changed her straw purse of the morning for a larger, leather one, which she now slipped off her bare shoulder and set on the bed. I watched her extract eight packets of crisp new bills, each bound with a paper wrapper. Her shoulders had a lovely soft slope to them. Her forearms looked strong but delicate and were covered with a light, golden down.

"I'm sorry. I didn't mean to snap."

She did not reply.

"Actually, you're not bad-looking yourself."

"Thanks," she said grudgingly.

I had a terrible urge to touch her.

"What I mean is, I think you're a knockout."

She smiled. Her teeth were dazzling.

"What do we do now?" she asked.

"Huh? Oh, now. Hmm." I tried to concentrate on the business at hand.

"Maybe you should count the money," she suggested.

"Good idea," I agreed.

She walked to the window and stood with her back to it, watching me as I sorted through the stacks of bills.

"You look familiar," she said. "Have I seen you someplace before?"

"I doubt it. I just got in from Detroit."

"My name's Roxanne."

"I know. You told me."

"What's yours?"

"Raven."

"Raven? Is that your first name or your last name?"

"Just Raven."

She laughed. "You mean like just Prince or just Madonna?"

"I mean like just Sparafucile."

"Spara who?"

"Spara-foo-chee-lay," I enunciated carefully. "The guy Rigoletto hired to kill the duke."

"Huh?"

I could tell by her blank look that she was no devotee of opera. It's hard to be a classy assassin in a world that has lost its culture.

"You don't know *Rigoletto?*" I asked.

She shook her head, pursing her lips and looking a little scared.

"Which family is he with?"

"Family?"

"Is he Mafia?"

"Nah. Just some clown."

"Oh." Her smile had become a trifle wan. She looked nervous.

"I hope I don't seem too edgy," she said. "I've never done anything like this before. Had a man killed, I mean."

"The first time's always the hardest."

"I guess you're used to it by now."

I shrugged modestly. "Murder doesn't mean anything to me."

"Do you like doing it?"

I shrugged again. "It's a living."

She had moved closer and was standing only a foot or so away, gazing at me thoughtfully. Her eyes had the deep, cool greenness of fern. I wanted to kiss them. I wanted to hold her in my arms.

"What's next?" she asked.

I thought it over.

"Maybe I should show you the photographs," she suggested.

"Photographs?"

"Of Johnny."

"Johnny? Who's Johnny?"

"You know, the, er . . ."

"Oh. Oh, yeah. Good idea."

She retrieved her purse and took out four photographs: three in color, one black and white. They were of a man in his mid-fifties, with a big, florid face, heavy eyebrows, and thick, black hair streaked with grey. He had a large nose that was not quite straight, as if it had been broken and not set right. Together with an imposing square jaw it gave him an appearance of toughness that was contradicted by his full, almost feminine lips and a dimple at the point of his chin. He had the look of a man well pleased with his lot in life.

"He looks kind of familiar," I said, as I studied the photograph. "Who is he?"

"His name is John Barany. He owns a restaurant in the East Fifties. The Budapest Nights."

"Oh! Oh, yeah. I know that place. I used to . . . er, I've eaten there a few times."

"Have you? Then you've probably seen him there."

I had almost let the truth slip that I had worked for several months as a waiter at the Budapest Nights. It was a small but fashionable place, favored by upper-level mobsters and well-to-do sports stars and pop music idols of a bygone generation. The tips had been tremendous.

"He also owns a chain of gourmet delicatessens and a frozen food company."

"Wow!" I exclaimed. "He must be a very rich man."

I did not even try to hide my excitement. I was being hired to kill a man of substance, practically a celebrity, someone you might expect to watch on "Lifestyles of the Rich and Famous." It was hard not to feel a touch of pride at having snared such a plum assignment so soon after entering the profession.

"What's the matter?" asked the blonde. "Does that make you nervous?"

"No, of course not," I answered hastily. "I just seem to remember hearing about him being a big philanthropist."

"He's a prick," she replied.

"Oh," I said.

"He deserves to die."

"I don't doubt it," I said. "I just remember reading about him throwing benefits to raise money for the opera and muscular dystrophy and things like that."

"He destroys whatever he gets his hands on."

"Well, they are a little heavy on the paprika in that place."

"If you won't do the job, I'll kill him myself."

Her tone was harsh and bitter.

"No, no. I'll take the job," I assured her.

"I'm not going to take a fall for him. I've got to look out for myself."

"Sure."

"I've been on my own since I was fourteen and it hasn't been any goddamn picnic."

"You can count on me," I said.

She seemed not to hear me. Tears were streaming down her cheeks, and she began to shiver.

"Hey, take it easy," I said. "Everything will be all right."

She covered her face with her hands and sobbed softly. She looked vulnerable and forlorn, and I felt a great surge of tenderness toward her.

"Uh, Roxanne."

I put my hands on her shoulders. She reacted by moving against me and burying her face in my chest.

"Oh Christ. Just hold me a little while."

I put my arms around her and held her close while she cried away whatever demon had possession of her. After a time she leaned her head back, away from my chest, and looked up at me. I kissed her lightly, once on each tear-stained cheek, then looked deep into her eyes.

"Oh God, I'm sorry," she said, dropping her gaze from mine. "I don't know what got into me. I don't often go to pieces like that."

"Roxanne . . ."

"No, don't say anything. Just lend me a handkerchief, okay?"

As I reached into my pocket she slipped from my grasp and took a backward step away from me. I handed her my handkerchief.

"Thanks," she said when she had wiped away her tears. "I'm sorry about what happened just now. I really am. If things were different between us, it might have been nice . . ."

Her voice trailed off. I waited for her to continue.

"But, things being what they are, I think it's best that we get back to business, don't you?"

She handed back my handkerchief. I sighed.

"Yeah, sure. I guess you're right."

"What do we do now?" she asked.

"Well, I guess that's it. We're finished. You wait here and give me a fifteen-minute start, then . . ."

"Wait a minute," she said. "How do I get in touch with you if I have to?"

"Get in touch with me? What would you need to do that for?"

"In case something goes wrong."

"Nothing will go wrong."

"I mean what if you miss or something? How do I get my money back?"

"I never miss."

"Well, that may be, but I'll feel a lot better if I know how to get in touch with you. After all, you're walking out of here with four thousand dollars of my money. I want to know how to find you if I have to."

She dug in her purse and came up with a little spiral notebook and a ball point pen.

"Here," she said, tearing out a page and handing it to me. "Why don't you write down a number where I can reach you?"

"Oh, for crying out loud."

I wrote down the number of the Chinese take-out place around the corner from my old apartment with Maud.

"Here," I said, a little peevishly. "Just ask for Raven."

"Thanks."

"How about you?" I asked. "How do I get in touch with you?"

"What for?"

"To collect the rest of the money."

"Oh."

She tore out another page and wrote down a number.

"Here," she said. "Just ask for Roxanne."

"I guess that's it, then."

"Don't you want me to tell you anything about Johnny? Like his schedule, where to find him? Things like that?"

"Oh, sure. Good idea."

For the next ten minutes she filled me in on some details, the various addresses—the apartment on Central Park West, the summer house at the Jersey shore —as well as up-to-date info on his habits and schedule. She seemed very well informed.

"He's out of town right now," she told me. "Gets back day after tomorrow. The sooner the better after that."

"Leave everything to me."

I picked up the attaché case and held it in my left hand as I extended my right to her. Instead of taking it, she moved in close to me and kissed me briefly on the lips.

"Good-bye, Raven," she said. "Thanks for holding me when I needed it."

"My pleasure," I replied.

"It's too bad we didn't meet in some other way. It could have been nice."

"It could have been wonderful," I said.

As I rode down in the elevator I pondered the chances of calling her up some day. After a long cooling-off period, of course. But by the time I reached ground level I realized what an impossible idea that was. Too bad, because she was really something special. It made me feel a little sad. I guess survival has its price.

5

The day was warm, and Phil Bender's apartment is down in the Village, but I decided to walk at least part of the way. I needed some exercise to burn off the extra adrenaline in my system and some gritty midtown air to rub the smell of disinfectant out of my nostrils. Not to mention the cheap thrill it gave me to walk down Seventh Avenue carrying four thousand dollars in small bills packed inside my attaché case.

But by the time I reached Forty-third Street the game had palled. My nerves were frayed. My shirt was glued to me with sweat. My feet hurt, my eyes ached, and a miasma of paranoia hovered around my head like a cloud of tobacco smoke.

I was sure I was being followed. A short, wiry man in a shiny, dark suit had been trailing half a block behind me since Forty-sixth Street. He had dark, greasy hair, a swarthy complexion, and sinister eyes. I stopped under a marquee just below Forty-third Street to see what he would do, watching him out of the corner of my eye as I pretended to study the promo pictures for the current double feature, *Lashed with Lust* and *Whip Me Tender*. He stopped in front of another movie house half a block up the street and watched me out of the corner of his eye as he pretended to study the poster advertising *Boys in Silk* and *Sweet Sodomy*.

At the corner of Forty-first Street a skinny teen-ager with a shaved head, cut-off tee shirt, and ring in his nose was hawking a line of imitation Rolex watches that were strapped up and down his sinewy arms. I pretended to admire them while sneaking glances over my shoulder at my swarthy pursuer. He pretended to be absorbed in the performance of a tall black man in a gold lamé dress lip synching a Sarah Vaughan ballad blasting from a huge Sanyo tape player on the ground behind him.

As I watched I became uncomfortably aware of a hand moving along the inside of my thigh. I tight-ened my grip on the attaché case and looked around. Dropping my gaze several feet I saw an emaciated boy grinning up at me as he caressed my leg. He could not have been over twelve.

I looked around wildly, spotted a taxi discharging a fare on the other side of Forty-first, and made a dash for it.

"Mercer Street," I gasped as I threw myself into the back seat.

As the cab pulled away I looked through the rear window. The kid had his hand on the leg of a plump, elderly man in an American Legion cap. The swarthy man who had been following me was nowhere in sight.

A touch of hysteria, I decided, brought on by taut nerves and an actor's overactive imagination. Noth-ing a hot bath and a cold gin-and-tonic wouldn't cure.

On the other hand, there was no point in taking chances. As the fellow said, just because you're para-noid doesn't mean they're not after you.

My answering machine held three messages from Jerry reminding me to call him as soon as I returned. Also one from Teresa on behalf of Morrie Ritz, with news of a tentative appointment for a probable audition for a possible part in a rumored TV commercial.

"For hemorrhoid suppositories." Teresa's giggle sounded tinny on the machine. "Not exactly Hamlet, but it pays. You even have a line. 'I can't sit down and I won't stand for it.' Morrie says to look like you're in pain when you deliver it."

"That won't be hard," I mumbled.

Four years of college plus a Master of Fine Arts. Eight years of acting classes, dancing classes, singing classes, fencing classes. Heartbreak and tears and the pain of rejection, all for that one big magic moment. A chance to simulate rectal itch.

I turned off the answering machine and was about to pick up the phone when it started to ring.

"How'd it go?" asked Jerry, not bothering with hello.

"Okay, I guess. She seemed to buy it even if it wasn't one of my better performances." I squeezed the receiver between my jaw and shoulder, leaving my hands free to loosen my tie and unbutton the top two buttons of my perspiration-soaked shirt. "Do you know who she wants me to kill?"

"Don't tell me," answered Jerry sharply.

"John Barany."

"I told you not to tell me." Then after a short pause, "Who's John Barany?"

"You know. The guy who owns the Budapest Nights, over on East Fifty-sixth Street."

"Oh, yeah. I know that place. It's a big hangout. Didn't Frank Sinatra once punch somebody there?"

"No, I think that was Billy Martin."

"Oh. Well, that's still a touch of distinction, don't you think? You really got hired for a first-class hit. You're a credit to the profession."

"Very funny, but it makes me nervous. Barany's got a lot of big-time friends."

"Yeah. Mafia connections, too. Or so I hear."

"Great. That makes me feel just great."

"Why? What do you care?"

"Well, he doesn't sound like a good guy to tangle with."

"So don't tangle with him. Don't dance with him at all."

He began to sing off key.

"It takes two to tangle, two to tangle . . ."

"For crying out loud, will you be serious? I just took four thousand dollars to murder the man."

"Sure. But you're not planning to do it, are you?"

"No, of course not, but . . ."

"No buts about it. You did the guy a favor, maybe even saved his life. That broad won't be so quick to put out another contract."

"I guess you're right. I just can't help feeling like a swindler."

"Of course you can't help feeling like a swindler. You *are* a swindler. What's that got to do with it?"

"Oh, nothing, I guess. It's just that she seemed so . . . I don't know . . . she seemed so nice."

"Elliot, she was hiring you to kill somebody. How nice can she be?"

"Yeah, I know."

"Good. Then let's skip it and get to the interesting part. Where's the money?"

"What do you mean, where is it? It's right here. When are you coming over to make the split?"

"Around ten or eleven o'clock."

"Can't you make it a little earlier? It makes me nervous having all that money around."

"Everything makes you nervous."

"Well, the place has been burglarized twice."

"Okay, okay. I'll make it as early as I can. I have a few things to take care of, then I'll come right over. Stash the money under the mattress until I get there, and try to relax."

Which is what I did, more or less. I pushed the attaché case—money, gun, and all—as far back under the bed as I could reach, then went back to the living room and mixed myself a tall gin-and-tonic. I took off my wet, wilted shirt, sat down barechested in front of the air conditioner, closed my eyes, and thought about Roxanne. Her image glowed in my inner eye— hair like sunbeams, vivid green eyes, generous pink mouth. By concentrating hard I made her lips part, curve widely in a broad smile, then silently mouth the words "I love you, Elliot." She looked so sweet as she said it, so genuine, so free of guile, it was hard to believe that only an hour before she had been engaged in buying my services as a murderer. I wondered what circumstances had driven her to such a desperate pass and whether I would ever see her again.

After a while I began to shiver. The air conditioner had done its job too well. The room felt about as cozy as a meat locker. Any further romantic reverie would have to take place in a hot shower.

Ten minutes under a warm spray and half a dozen choruses of "What I Did for Love" did wonders for my state of mind. I was ready to tackle another gin-and-tonic. Maybe even think about dinner. As I reached for a towel the phone began to ring.

Let it ring, thought I. Let the answering machine get it. Mr. Fenway is not taking calls tonight. No, tonight he is going to celebrate the conclusion of a most successful engagement by having another drink and then taking his good friend Mr. Elliot Feinstein out for a steak dinner.

"That's nice of you, Elliot," said Feinstein, "but what about your career? What if Joseph Papp caught the whisper of tragic nobility you breathed into the part of the gigolo in "A Brighter Tomorrow" and is calling to offer you the lead in his coming production of *Hamlet?* Or Stephen Sondheim, so taken with your impersonation of a dancing banana that he wants to cast you as a singing still life in his new musical version of the works of Cézanne. Can you afford to let him talk to a machine?"

Fenway and Feinstein glared at each other for a split second, during which the telephone rang for the third time. Then, wrapping a towel around their joint waist, they jumped from the tub and ran pell-mell to the living room, where they tripped on the carpet and fell against the base of Phil Bender's top-dollar imitation Tiffany lamp.

"Hello?"

Poised in a three-quarter split, I steadied the lamp with one hand and juggled the telephone with the other.

"Hello," said a voice on the other end. "Is this Raven?"

I felt as if a hand had reached out of the receiver and whacked me hard on the side of the head.

"Hello, is this Raven?" the voice repeated.

"Who is this?" I managed to croak. My mouth felt as if I had just eaten a cobweb.

"It's Roxanne," she answered, as casually as if she phoned me every day. "I called to say I changed my mind."

"How did you find me?" I felt a sudden, irrational fear of the telephone receiver, as if it were possessed with a malevolent consciousness. I held it nearly a foot from my face and peered at it out of the corner of my eye.

"It doesn't matter how I found you." Her voice sounded far away and had a sinister, metallic ring. "The point is, I don't want you to do the job."

"How did you find me?" I repeated dully.

"Hello? I think something's happened to the connection. You sound awfully far away."

I brought the phone back to normal position.

"You followed me, didn't you?" I spoke loudly, right into the mouthpiece.

"Now you're too loud," she complained.

"You followed me from the hotel disguised as a swarthy man with sinister eyes, didn't you?"

"What are you talking about?"

"Or maybe you were the tall black guy doing the Sarah Vaughn imitation. Or the kid with the watches."

"I don't know what you're talking about. You sound kind of crazy."

"How did you find me?" I screamed into the phone.

"Well, if you must know, it was that book. You left it in the hotel room."

"Book?"

"You know, the one you were carrying around. What's it called? Wait a minute. Oh, yeah. *This Gun for Hire.*"

"I left it in the hotel room?"

"Yes. There was a letter inside addressed to you. Philip J. Bender, 180 Mercer Street. I looked up the number in the book."

"Oh."

"The letter was from Consolidated Edison. You owe them two months' back bills."

"Oh."

"I guess the assassin business must be kind of slow in the summer."

"I . . . uh . . . I've had a lot of expenses."

"Who hasn't?" she said sympathetically. "Well, I hate to add to your problems, but I've changed my mind."

"What do you mean, you've changed your mind? You can't change your mind just like that."

"Why not?"

"Why not?" I repeated. "Because it just isn't done, that's why. It isn't right."

"Well, of course, I hate to commit a breach of etiquette. It's just that I've decided to take care of things another way."

"Another way? What have you been doing, comparison shopping?"

She sighed. "Look, Phil . . . you don't mind if I call you Phil, do you?"

I ignored the question.

"The thing is, Phil, I don't want to hurt your feelings or anything, but I don't have much confidence in your ability to do the job."

"Not much confidence? What are you talking about? Listen, lady . . ."

"Oh, come on, Phil. You're about as convincing a hit man as Mr. Rodgers."

I was too hurt to reply.

"Then I began to think maybe you were setting me up."

"Setting you up?" I looked around the apartment for someplace to hide when the bunco squad arrived.

"You know, some kind of con game. Oh, not that I think you're a professional con man or anything like that. More like an amateur."

That hurt even more. I hate amateurs.

"For all I know," she went on, "you could even be some actor, down on his luck, trying to make a quick buck."

"An actor? Don't make me laugh."

"Well, maybe not a real actor like Laurence Olivier or Arnold Schwarzenegger. More like one of those daytime TV types."

"What are you talking about? Some of the best actors in New York work the soaps."

"Do they? I wouldn't know. I only know I want my money back. I've decided to handle things my own way."

"You mean you want a refund?"

"Of course I want a refund. I just cancelled the job, didn't I?"

"You can't get a refund."

"Why not?"

"Because it just isn't done."

"Of course it's done," she insisted. "It's done all the time. Every store in New York gives refunds."

"Oh, yeah? Well, not many of them sell murder

contracts. At least I didn't see any the last time I was in Bloomingdale's."

There was a short pause; then she spoke in a determined voice.

"Phil, I don't want to make trouble for you, but I'll go to the police if I have to."

"And tell them what? That you hired me to kill John Barany? Don't make me laugh."

She was silent.

"It looks like a standoff to me," I said.

"I have some friends who can make things tough for you."

I did not reply.

"I wouldn't, er, lean on you like this if I wasn't desperate," she said. Her voice sounded choked. "I'm really in big trouble. I don't know how long I can . . ."

She broke off. I thought for a moment the line was dead.

"Hey, are you all right?"

There was a long silence.

"I, uh . . . Raven, give me a break."

She sounded very forlorn.

"Maybe we can work something out," I said.

"I'd really appreciate it."

"Maybe a partial refund. I have to talk to my, er, partner first. Why don't you call me tomorrow around this time."

"Sure."

I could hear the relief in her voice.

"Maybe we could have dinner together and work things out," I suggested.

"That would be nice. Oh, and Phil . . ."

There was a decidedly upbeat note in her voice.

"Yes?"

"Swindler or not, I still think you're cute."

I tried to weigh that against the loss of a couple of thousand dollars.

"Oh, and Phil . . ."

There was no question she had made a quick recovery.

"Yes?"

"I tried that phone number you gave me."

"Oh."

"I really prefer pizza. Do you know any places that deliver?"

Before I could think of an answer she had hung up. I wished I had remembered to ask her about returning *This Gun for Hire*. I hadn't finished reading it, and I wanted to see how Raven handled women.

6

After my conversation with Roxanne I gave up the idea of going out for dinner and settled for half a can of tuna fish and a sliced tomato at home. There didn't seem to be much to celebrate.

Roxanne was on to me. She knew I was no professional killer, not even an amateur of decent standing. In fact, she suspected me of being what I was—an out-of-work actor. And what that said about my hopes for success in a metier requiring suspension of disbelief as a *sine qua non* was something I did not care to consider on half a can of tuna fish and a sliced tomato. I tried to console myself by listing the handicaps I had worked under—inadequate set, poor lighting, no makeup. Not to mention lack of rehearsal and the barest outline of a script. Even Alfred Lunt had limitations.

She wanted her money back, and she knew where to find me. That was the nub of it and it rankled. I tried to tell myself that money wasn't everything but was unable to give a convincing reading of the line. *He who steals my purse steals trash* is all very well for the likes of Iago, but he didn't have to cope with New York rents. Nor did he have a partner in crime like Jerry De Marco, who could be expected to receive the suggestion of returning the loot with all the grace of John McEnroe accepting a double-fault call.

But what could I do? She had found me out. And even if she was not in a position to go to the police, I had lost the advantage of being an anonymous heel. It's hard to swindle someone who knows where you live.

Well, there was still the prospect of a TV commercial to cheer me up, so for the next half-hour I revived my failing spirits by concentrating on hemorrhoid suppositories.

"I can't sit down, and I won't stand for it!" I told my reflection in the little mirror above the commode, starting with an attitude of mild indignation and working my way through several readings to a state of barely suppressed rage.

After that I indulged in a quarter-hour fantasy, a satisfying little scenario that opened with me sweeping the audition, going on to win an Emmy for best performance in a nonprescription medicine commercial, then moving through a succession of highly lucrative guest appearances to the lead in a prime-time series and a starring role opposite Meryl Streep in a major motion picture. My Academy Award acceptance speech was interrupted by a pounding on the door.

"Who is it?" I cried, trying to get a gander at my caller through the little peephole. Phil's apartment door has one of those fish-eye things that is supposed to give you a sweeping view of the entire hallway, with the person on the other side of the door looking like a Munchkin with dropsy. But the one on Phil's door must have been designed by a minimalist, because all I can ever see through it are various shades of white.

"Who is it?" I repeated.

"Police!"

"I beg your pardon?"

"Police. Open up. We want to talk to you about Roxanne Adair."

"Roxanne Adair?"

"Yeah. The woman you were with this afternoon in the Hotel Clayton."

My stomach jumped through my throat and out onto the floor where it began running laps around the perimeter of the living room.

"Come on, Bender, open up." The voice was nasal and whiny and merciless as a dentist's drill. "Don't make more trouble for yourself than you already got."

I unbolted the door and opened it about two inches, keeping the chain lock in place. There were two men standing in the hallway. The one in front was short, not more than five-five, and very slender. He looked about thirty years old and was dressed for success in a beautifully fitted, shiny grey lightweight suit. He smiled up at me, exuding self-assurance as he held out a wallet opened to display a police badge. His smile revealed a set of pointy little teeth that any piranha would have been proud to own.

"Why make trouble for yourself?" he asked in the voice of a snake about to strike. "We only want to talk to you."

The man behind him was older, maybe forty, and a good foot taller than his companion, with big shoulders and a very prominent jaw. His face had a fatty droop that gave him the look of a retired linebacker gone to seed doing beer commercials but still capable of breaking the occasional arm or leg.

"You're welcome to come in, officers," I said, slipping the chain from its hasp, "though I don't really understand what you want with me."

I had not decided how to play the scene—outraged innocence or monolithic ignorance or naivete flavored with a soupcon of contrition—but it did not matter, for the lead was taken away from me the moment I unchained the door. The smaller man slid through the opening without perceptibly widening it, and his oversized mate bulled in behind him. No sooner had the big fellow slammed the door than they both had guns in their hands, and of a size that would surely have satisfied Roxanne Adair's standards of professionalism.

"Up against the wall and keep your arms over your head," whined Piranha-mouth as his partner spun me around and shoved me forward.

"Hey!" I shouted. "What do you think you're doing? You have no right to—"

"Shut up," growled the big guy, speaking for the first time. His voice had the lilt of a hundred chain saws. He held his gun close to my face while his partner patted me up and down the length of my body.

"He's clean," whined shorty after his hands had finished their *pas de deux* around my torso. "Hold on to him while I check out the rest of the apartment."

"Wait a minute!" My anger pushed my voice a few decibels above normal volume; my fear raised the pitch about an octave and a half. "You can't search my apartment without a warrant. And who gave you the right to—"

"Shut up," said the big man. It seemed to be a favorite locution of his. This time he punctuated it by grabbing my wrist and twisting my arm behind my back. A searing pain roared up my arm like an express train, ran across my shoulder, through my neck and into my head, where it slammed against the top of my skull, reversed course and made the return trip back down to my fingers.

"Shut up," he repeated, without waiting for me to say anything.

"There's not much to this apartment, is there?" said the short man, emerging from the bedroom. "What do you pay for a place like this?"

My arm was numb, my heart felt like it was welded to my Adam's apple, and fear flowed like the Colorado River through my intestines. But my sense of outrage refused to be squelched.

"I want your badge numbers," I said through clenched teeth.

"Our what?"

"Your badge numbers. I intend to report this to the commissioner's office. You guys picked on the wrong person this time. You're not going to brutalize me and get away with it."

The big man began to laugh. It sounded like a barrel falling off a truck.

"He wants your badge number, Vinnie."

"Oh, my *badge* number," said the other. He grinned as if he had just eaten a tankful of guppies. "My badge is number double-oh-seven. You can call me James."

"I'm glad you find this so funny," I said indignantly. "It will be interesting to see if the police review board . . ."

I stopped in mid-sentence. Reality grabbed hold of me like a stomach cramp.

"You're not cops," I said.

"Ah, you guessed our secret." He grinned again.

"But you said you were cops."

"Sometimes we fib a little. Everybody does. It makes life easier."

"What do you want with me?" Now I was really scared. "Is it the money? You can have it. I was planning to give it back."

"Shhh. Calm down," said Vinnie. "Don't get so excited."

"What do you mean, don't get so excited? I want to know what's going on. You force your way in here, rough me up, hold me at gunpoint . . ."

"You make too much noise," he admonished me. "You're a raven, aren't you? Ravens aren't supposed to sing."

"Yeah," said his partner. "Just croak."

He chuckled. It sounded like a bowling ball falling down a flight of stairs.

"Let's get going," said Vinnie. His partner gripped my right arm and twisted it behind my back.

"Going? Going where?" I asked. "I'm not going anywhere."

"Raven, do me a favor," said Vinnie in a reasonable tone, while his henchman squeezed the juice out of my forearm. "Don't give us a hard time. It's been a long day. Just come along like a good boy and don't make us get mean. And be nice and quiet when we're down in the street, okay? No screaming, no shouting for help, kapeesh? Otherwise Muzio here will have to do something bad."

"Yeah," said Muzio. "Then there'll be one less raven to shit on the statues." He twisted my arm for emphasis. Ravens don't shit on the statues, you asshole, I thought. It's pigeons that shit on the statues. But I decided he wasn't worth educating.

Their car was a huge Lincoln Continental. Black, naturally. I had the eerie feeling I was acting in a gangster movie. None of it seemed real. There was dapper little Vinnie with the piranha teeth and classy lightweight suit, and big ugly Muzio with the tight plaid jacket and sociopathic chuckle. Early John Huston, perhaps, or maybe Francis Ford Coppola.

"Hey, is this some kind of gag?" I asked them breathlessly, as they hustled me into the back seat of the car. Neither man responded.

"Tell me the truth, are you guys actors?"

"Watch your language," said Muzio, giving my arm a twist. The pain made my teeth quiver.

Vinnie drove. Muzio and I shared the back seat.

"Seriously, fellows, what's going on? I mean, what could you guys possibly want with me?"

There was no answer.

"Could you at least give me some idea what time we'll be back? I have an important audition tomorrow, and I'd like to get a good night's sleep. Also, I'm supposed to call my agent. In fact, I should have already called him. He's probably out scouring the city for me right now."

"Shut up," replied Muzio.

We rode in silence, moving south and east across lower Manhattan, through a sluggish stream of traffic on Chambers Street, past the Criminal Courts Building, then up onto the Brooklyn Bridge.

"Could you turn down the air-conditioning a little?" I asked the back of Vinnie's head. "It's kind of cold in here."

He made no move to adjust the controls.

"Thanks," I said, scrunching my body as tight as I could and rubbing my hands up and down my arms for warmth. I wished I had brought a sweater with me. I wished I had gone to California with Phil. I wished I had been born in another century.

"I guess we're going to Brooklyn," I said as we rode down the exit ramp from the bridge. "I have an aunt in Brooklyn. Out near Sheepshead Bay. You think we'll be going that way?"

No response.

"Ida Horowitz, my father's sister. Of course, Horowitz is her married name. Her original name was Ida Feinstein."

I realized as soon as I said it I had made a slip.

"Did I say Feinstein? I meant Bender. Ida Bender. Why on earth did I say Feinstein? It must be because of this big audition I have tomorrow. It's making me nervous. Or maybe I'm just delirious from hypothermia."

Muzio stared at me, dumb and impassive as an ox.

"It's your line," I told him. "You're supposed to say shut up."

"Shut up," he replied.

I gave up trying to maintain my end of the conversation and thought about John Huston movies. *The Maltese Falcon*, the scene where Bogie takes the gun away from the little hood played by Elisha Cook, Jr. Only they were on foot and we were in a car. And Bogie had only one hood to deal with whereas I had two. And Muzio wasn't Elisha Cook, Jr. And I wasn't Bogie.

We went past a high-rise complex and turned onto a broad shopping street, now largely deserted. Then through a neighborhood of brownstone houses into a section where warehouses and garages blended with seedy tenements. At last we pulled into a small parking lot adjoining a two-story, red-brick building.

"Out," said Muzio, a man of few words.

The building alongside the parking lot was the only structure on the block that did not look dilapidated. From its facade protruded a pair of large torches, burning with bright orange flame. Between the torches, black metal letters affixed to the wall spelled out the name TOZZI'S. Through the entranceway, as Vinnie pulled open the dark wooden door, came the din of a sizeable crowd of people, a chaotic mixture of dozens of disjoint conversations that blended into a stream of unintelligible conviviality. It was a friendly sound of which I felt badly in need.

We entered a dim-lit anteroom. Straight ahead, in an alcove bordered by a black wrought-iron fence, stood a gigantic fountain—six levels of plaster scallop shells catching jets of water colored by dancing beams of aqua, rose, and chartreuse lights. On our right was an unmanned hatcheck booth, and beyond it an archway through which there came a hubbub of voices and a steamy aroma of spices and garlic and cooking oil. To our left a staircase curved up into darkness.

Vinnie started up the stairs, and Muzio, by means of a viselike grip on my left shoulder and a pistol jammed into the small of my back, conveyed the suggestion that I follow along. At the top was a tiny landing with a single closed door. Vinnie knocked three times.

"Who's there?" demanded a gruff voice from within.

"Me, Vinnie. Open up."

After a short pause a key turned in the lock and the

door was opened. Vinnie slid into the room and Muzio pushed me along behind.

"Here he is," said Vinnie, waving a hand toward me. "The assassin."

7

Muzio closed the door and stood with his back against it, gun in hand. I took a long, slow, frightened look around what appeared to be a private dining room. The place was lit by fluorescent lights set behind a cornice on each of the side walls. What my mother used to call indirect lighting, in a tone that conferred a high degree of class. There were no windows.

At the far end of the room, seven men were sitting at a large horseshoe-shaped table covered with a white tablecloth and enough food to accommodate the cast of a Fellini movie. All of them faced me with hard stares. On the wall behind them hung a huge painting in a heavy, ornate gold frame; an immense seascape depicting a tiny boat storm-tossed amid waves of bilious blue-green topped with white spume. I knew how the boat felt.

The central figure in the group was a broad, squat man of about sixty with a large bald head, barrel chest, and no visible neck. One of his fat, hairy hands held a silver ladle over a large tureen filled with what looked, from where I stood, like fish heads swimming in thick, brown slime.

Next to him on his right was a much younger man who appeared in every way his opposite—slim and stylish, with tightly curled chestnut hair and narrow brown eyes that stared at me through tinted aviator glasses. He had a cool, intelligent air that set him apart from the rest of that company and made it look as if he had wandered in by mistake on his way to a Dartmouth reunion.

On the other side of Kid Dartmouth was a huge man in his sixties, built like a telephone booth. His head had the size, shape, and delicacy of an eight-cylinder engine, and a linen napkin was tucked daintily into the size-24 collar of his white dress shirt. One of his huge, raw paws grasped a fork, the other a tablespoon, both pointed tensely upward as if ready to disembowel an enemy.

Next to him, hunched over with his chin almost touching his dish of pasta, sat a man of about the same age, small and sharp-featured, with a thin black moustache and straight black hair that looked like a toupee. He peered at me over his plate as he shoveled a forkful of spaghetti into his mouth.

At the other end of the table sat a much older man, maybe eighty years old, with fine white hair and skin that had the dull, almost translucent look of stone worn smooth by centuries of handling. A classical profile—high, smooth forehead and large, aquiline nose—and rigid, immobile posture that gave him the look of something chiseled out of Carrara marble by some ancient sculptor. There was no food on the table in front of him, only a demitasse cup sitting in a tiny saucer.

On either side of the old man, erect, impassive and attentive, sat two much younger men, whose size made Muzio look positively dainty by comparison. They were as alike as the towers of the World Trade

Center, and radiated about the same degree of human warmth.

The only other person in the room was a little weasel-like creature perched gingerly on a chair in a corner of the room. I could have sworn it was indeed Elisha Cook, Jr., aged a bit since the Maltese Falcon caper and even more nervous.

The heavy silence was broken only by the sound of spaghetti being slurped by the little man with the mustache and toupee. I felt called upon to say something.

"Look here," I said, "I think there's been some mistake." A sound like an engine knock came from the eight-cylinder head. "You fellows must have me mixed up with somebody else," I added weakly.

"Shut up," replied the squat man with hairy hands. Muzio's speech teacher, obviously. "Sit down over there." He pointed to the row of chairs along the side wall. Vinnie guided me to a seat and sat down beside me. I decided not to protest, mostly because the fear constricting my throat made it hard to speak.

"This the guy?" He pointed a hairy finger at me. The question was apparently directed at Elisha Cook, Jr., who cleared his throat before answering.

"Y-y-yes, sir, Mr. Tarabola. Th-that's him, all right."

He seemed very edgy, eager to please the man with hairy hands. "He met the girl up on Riverside Drive this morning, then later in the hotel."

Mr. Tarabola turned his gaze on me.

"Well? What's your story?"

"I don't know what he's talking about," I answered.

The squat man curled his lip. "Play him some of that tape," he instructed Elisha Cook, Jr.

Next to the nervous little guy was a serving cart on which sat a tape player. Elisha took a cassette from his jacket pocket and inserted it in the machine.

Maybe I could think it over? A woman's voice, distant and fuzzy. The next sentence or two were obliterated by traffic noises, but I thought I made out the phrase *some time next week.*

By next week I might be in Palermo. A male voice, vaguely familiar. The recording was not of high quality. The voice trailed off and was covered by more traffic sounds.

"Play the other one," said Hairy-hands. "The one from the hotel."

He spooned a fish head out of the slime while Elisha fiddled with the machine.

Raven? A woman's voice, very clear. *Is that your first name or last name?*

Just Raven. A male voice, all too clear.

You mean like just Prince or just Madonna? Laughter.

I mean like just Sparafucile.

Spara who?

Spara-foo-chee-lay. The guy that Rigoletto hired to kill the duke.

"That's enough," said Hairy-hands. He picked his teeth with a fingernail while his underling removed the cassette from the machine.

"Well?" he said finally. "What have you got to say?"

I cleared my throat.

"That last part is certainly much clearer. Much better quality recording than the first, I would say."

"What are you, a comedian?" he asked coldly.

I cleared my throat again.

"Oh, uh, no. No, indeed. I, uh . . . I just don't understand what's going on."

He stared at me in hostile silence, a silence that was broken by the sound of a discreet cough from the old, white-haired gent with the aquiline nose. Everyone turned and looked at him with respectful attention.

"*Rigoletto* was my mother's favorite opera," he said softly.

He looked at me and smiled dreamily.

"My sainted mother, may her soul rest in peace."

He crossed himself. The two gorillas flanking him crossed themselves. The man with the hairy hands spat out a fishbone and crossed himself. Elisha Cook, Jr. and Kid Dartmouth and Enginehead and the man with the toupee all crossed themselves. Out of the corner of my eye I caught a glimpse of Muzio crossing himself with his pistol.

From that orgy of crossing only I stood aloof. I might have joined in just to play it safe, but I got confused about whether to go left-to-right or right-to-left, and before I had it figured out it was all over.

"This here," said the man with the hairy hands after a few moments of respectful silence, "is the top electronic surveillance expert in the city." He spoke to his colleagues at the table, gesturing at the nervous little fellow in the corner. "Maybe in the world. Ain't that so, Alfred?"

"Uh, the n-name is Albert, Mr. Tarabola. Albert Lemay." The little man smiled modestly. "I don't know about best in the world, but we get the job done. If you can say it we can hear it. That's like our motto."

I rated it about on a par with "I can't sit down and I won't stand for it."

"Like I mentioned before," Tarabola said to the others at the table, "Alfred here has been keeping an eye on the girl for the last week or so. Now, Alfred, take one more look at this comedian." He jabbed a hairy digit in my direction. "Make it a good look so that you're sure he's the guy you followed home this afternoon."

The little guy walked over and peered at me.

"Th-that's him, all right. He met the girl in the park this morning."

"He's the one she hired to knock off my friend John Barany?"

"Yes, sir. Only she didn't hire him right there in the park. They made arrangements to meet later in the hotel. H-H-Hotel Clayton, room 311." He looked very pleased with himself. "So I beat it d-down there and rented room 309."

"That was smart, Alfred. Quick thinking."

"Uh, Albert, Mr. Tarabola. Th-thanks."

"What happened to the girl?" The man with the toupee managed to ask the question while slurping spaghetti. The edge of his moustache was tinged with tomato sauce.

"I, uh, lost her. I c-couldn't follow both of them."

"That's okay, Alfred. Don't worry about it. Go on downstairs and have something to eat. And make sure they give you some cigars."

Tarabola made a gesture of dismissal, but Albert gave no indication of leaving. He stood in place, shifting his weight from one foot to the other.

"I, uh, d-don't smoke, Mr. Tarabola."

"Well, have 'em wrap up some pastry for your wife."

Lemay continued to fidget, looking uncomfortable.

"That's very nice of you, Mr. Tarabola, but I'm a little w-w-worried about how I should report this."

At the world "report" Tarabola's face darkened.

"Forget about any report," he said.

"Wh-what I mean is, this could be serious b-business. A m-murder contract and all."

"I said forget about any report."

"It's j-just that I'm worried about g-getting my license suspended again."

Tarabola reddened. He jabbed his index finger at Tarabola. "You listen to me—"

"Frank, if you'll permit me." Kid Dartmouth placed a restraining hand on the other's arm. He smiled at the little surveillance expert. "Now, Albert, you do a lot of work for my firm, don't you?"

He spoke in a soft but precise voice, the tone of a New England prep school headmaster admonishing a recalcitrant pupil. Albert looked at him sheepishly.

"It ain't that I d-don't appreciate everything, Mr. Nero. It's j-just that . . ."

"I think you can trust us to protect your interests. Mr. Tarabola forgot to mention that there will be a handsome bonus for your good work."

Lemay remained silent. Nero smiled at him placidly, his face betraying no emotion.

"It's understandable that you are worried about your license, but I assure you there is nothing to worry about. We will take care of everything very discreetly. Mr. Giusti here is a personal friend of the commissioner."

He indicated the white-haired gent at the far end of the table. All eyes turned in that direction. The old man sat erect in his chair, his eyes closed and his face fixed in a serene expression, making small motions with his two forefingers as if conducting some sweet strain of celestial music. Suddenly he stopped and opened his eyes, as if awakened by the stares focused upon him. He looked around in confusion, then bowed his head in a courtly manner.

"G-G-Giusti?" Albert Lemay's voice registered awe. "Eraldo Giusti?"

"The same," answered Nero.

"D-Don Eraldo Giusti?"

Nero nodded. The old man sat up stiffly and looked warily around.

"It's a great honor to meet you, Don Eraldo," said Lemay reverently. "My wife's f-father used to work for you when you had the trucking company on Sackett Street right after the war. T-Teddy Kopinski, you remember him? He used to drive a bulldog Mack."

Don Eraldo relaxed. He nodded serenely.

"I remember him. Big Polack, always making jokes."

"That's him," said Lemay excitedly.

"Tell him I said hello."

"He's d-dead, Don Eraldo."

"Oh. Too bad. Leave the address. I will send flowers."

"He d-died fifteen years ago, Don Eraldo."

The Don shook his head sadly.

"It doesn't matter. I will send flowers anyway." He sighed wistfully. "May his soul rest in peace."

I braced myself for another round of crossing, but before it could get under way the man named Nero resumed speaking in his headmaster voice.

"So you see, Albert, everything will be taken care of. You don't need to make a report."

"Whatever you say, Mr. Nero." He turned to

Hairy-hands. "I didn't mean to get out of line, Mr. Tarabola. No offence."

"Forget it, Alfred. Tell 'em downstairs I said to give you a whole box of cigars. Top quality, you'll like 'em."

No one spoke until the little man had left the room. Then Don Eraldo coughed softly. All eyes turned to him.

"Yes, Don Eraldo?" prompted Tarabola.

The old man remained silent for almost a full minute, staring into space, seemingly lost in thought. Then he turned to Tarabola.

"*La Traviata* was also a favorite of my mother. A very touching story. So sad."

There was a long silence while a tear rolled down the Don's cheek. It was broken by a rumble from the man with the eight-cylinder head.

"I told you right from the start, Frank, not to get mixed up with that Hungarian."

"That's right," said his smaller colleague. "Them people got no morals."

Frank Tarabola reddened. "What do you want, for Chrissake? The guy's married to my niece."

Enginehead shrugged disdainfully. "That don't cut no ice with me."

"Yeah," agreed the man with the tomato-stained moustache. "Besides, I heard your niece is dumping him for some nightclub comedian."

"That's a lot of bullshit," said Tarabola emphatically.

"Nightclub comedian?"

The words were out of my mouth before I realized what I was doing. They all fell silent and stared at me in a surprised way, as if they had just been reminded of my existence.

"Son of a bitch," growled Tarabola. "What the hell are we going to do with him?"

"What indeed?" asked Nero.

They looked at each other, then back at me.

"I remember in 1954 we had an accountant named Brodsky. Harold Brodsky." Don Eraldo's voice had an otherworldly quality, as if it came from far away. "We heard he was going to talk to the crime commission, so we buried him in the foundation of a housing project in Astoria."

He smiled benignly at me.

"Sealed up in a tomb. Like Aida. So sad."

8

I dreamed of Don Eraldo throughout that night. The benign smile, the sad eyes following me as I ran up endless stairways toward some light that kept receding, the words *a housing project in Astoria* ringing in my ears. Sometimes the features would blur, shifting and rearranging themselves to form the mean little face of Vinnie, his piranha teeth moist with excitement.

Two or three times I woke to find the pillowcase wet with perspiration and a lump of fear lying like an ice cube in my stomach. Then a warm sense of relief would flood through me like a spring thaw at the realization I was dreaming. Maybe, I told myself hopefully, it had all been a dream—the ride to Brooklyn, the fish heads, the old man who smiled so sweetly as he told of burying accountants in concrete. But the pain in my arm where Muzio had twisted it was definitely real, and so was the deep purple bruise he had left on my wrist.

They had questioned me for over an hour.

"Who are you?"

"An actor." I had decided my best course lay in telling the truth, at least when I was unable to think of any plausible lie that would serve any better.

"What's your name?"

"Elliot Fenway."

"How did you get mixed up in this?"

"It was just a dumb idea to make money."

"You mean a scam?"

"I guess so. I should have known better. I'm not the type."

"Where'd you meet the broad?"

"In a bar."

"Who was with you?"

"Nobody. It was just me and her."

I had decided not to mention Jerry De Marco if I could help it. Not that I felt I owed him anything. If Willie's reference to a nightclub comedian meant who I thought it did, then Jerry had not been completely honest with me, to say the least. Still and all, I didn't want to be overwhelmed with remorse every time I passed a construction site.

"What's the name of the bar you met her in?"

"It's near Columbus Circle. I forget the name."

And so it went, over and over, until at last, to my great surprise, they let me go with fearsome warnings to keep my mouth shut and reminders that they knew where to find me.

"Behave yourself, actor," Tarabola had told me grimly. "We'll be keeping an eye on you."

"And if you want a little advice, stick to your own trade," added young Nero sardonically. "Don't try to steal the bread out of another man's mouth."

Vinnie and Muzio even drove me home, although, as someone once said about being tarred and feathered and ridden out of town on a rail, if it hadn't been for the honor of the thing I'd have just as soon walked. But it was late, I didn't know my way home, and I didn't want to be accused of any breach of underworld etiquette.

On the ride back to Manhattan Muzio kept staring at me, frowning and wrinkling his brow as if grappling with some mental problem way beyond his abilities, such as the harder sections of the multiplication table. Suddenly, his face brightened.

"Hey! I know you!" he said delightedly. "You're the guy who knocked up Lisa Duncan."

"I beg your pardon?"

"You know. Dr. Todd Duncan's wife."

"Oh, you're talking about 'A Brighter Tomorrow.' "

His face assumed an earnest, troubled look.

"What would ever make a good-looking broad like that become a lez?"

"I, uh, really don't know her all that well," I said.

"It's a shame. Ain't it, Vinnie?" he asked his partner. "About Lisa Duncan being a dyke, I mean."

"Who's Lisa Duncan?" asked Vinnie.

"That hot-looking blonde on 'A Brighter Tomorrow,' " Muzio answered.

"I never watch it," said Vinnie flatly. "It's on the same time as 'All Our Yesterdays.' "

He double-parked in front of my building.

"You're lucky, Raven. Don't let it go to your head. Remember we know where to find you."

The first thing I did on entering my apartment was to fall on my knees and kiss the floor. The second was to call Jerry De Marco. The phone rang eleven times before it was answered.

"Hello," said a sleepy female voice.

"Gloria? It's me, Elliot. I'm sorry to wake you, but I have to talk to Jerry."

"Elliot? Uh, what time is it?"

I looked at the clock next to the bed. "Around midnight."

"Gee, are you all right? I mean is something wrong?"

"No, no, everything's fine. I just have to talk to Jerry."

"Oh. Well, he isn't here."

"Oh."

"He's never here."

I didn't know how to respond to that.

"I mean we don't see much of each other. I'm working all day and Jerry's never home at night. He's always got to see some guy or do some shtick."

"Oh."

"You know how it is."

"Sure."

"So, how you been?"

"Oh, great. Just great. How about you?"

"Well, not so good."

"Oh. I'm sorry to hear that." Then I remembered what Jerry had told me. "Hey, does it have anything to do with your operation?"

"Operation?"

"Jerry told me you were having an operation."

"Oh, that. I had it this morning."

"And Jerry left you alone? Isn't anybody staying with you? Why aren't you in the hospital?"

"Elliot, for heaven's sake, it was only a plantar's wart. I have them removed all the time."

"Oh. Then what's wrong?"

There was a pause.

"It's just me and Jerry," she said. "Things are pretty bad between us. I mean, I think we're in real trouble as far as the marriage is concerned."

"Oh. I'm sorry to hear that."

"I sent Gary to Montana to stay with my parents for the summer while I think things out. I don't want him to be caught in the middle, you know what I mean?"

"Sure. Look, Gloria, could you leave Jerry a note?"

"Elliot, do you think we could get together one of these days? Maybe for lunch or something? I could use somebody to talk to."

"Sure. I'll call you soon. In the meantime could you please leave Jerry a message to get in touch with me right away? I mean right away. I don't care what time it is. It's very important."

"I don't know why I didn't fall in love with you, Elliot. It would have been much smarter."

"I guess I wasn't the right type. That's what they're always telling me."

"You're sweet, Elliot. The sweetest guy I know."

"Thanks, Gloria. In the meantime, could you please leave Jerry a note that I have to talk to him right away? It's very important."

"Sure. I'll tape it on the mirror. That's the one place I'm sure he'll look."

After that conversation I went to sleep. *To sleep: perchance to dream: ay, there's the rub*, says Shakespeare. And he never even met the gang at Tozzi's restaurant.

What with tossing and turning and dreaming and waking I passed a very restless night, and it wasn't until morning that I managed to get a bit of uninterrupted sleep. It must have been close to six o'clock. Light was spilling around the edges of the Venetian blinds. I pulled the covers over my head, curled my body up tight, and surrendered myself to the sweet sensation of numbness that came over me.

Minutes later, or so it seemed, the telephone started to ring.

"Rise and shine, Elliot! Great news!"

It was Teresa Gianelli, my guardian angel and number-one fan at the Morrie Ritz graveyard of talent, sounding much too chipper for the way I felt.

"What kind of great news could there be at this hour?" I asked irritably.

"Hour?" There was a nauseatingly cheery lilt to her voice. "It's ten-thirty, Elliot. The rest of the world has already been working for an hour or two."

I squinted at the alarm clock for corroboration.

"Now listen," she went on excitedly. "Splash some cold water on your face and get dressed in a hurry because you have an appointment in exactly one hour with a movie producer."

"Movie producer?"

"Uh-huh. Appian Productions. They called here looking for you. Isn't that wonderful? It's not like Morrie had to call them and try to sell you to them. They want you!"

"Appian Productions?" I tried to place the name.

"It's a new outfit, just formed out on the coast. They're only in town for a few days, casting for a remake of *Ben Hur*." Teresa was breathless. "Elliot, they're interested in you for the lead!"

"*Ben Hur?*"

"Uh-huh. Look, there's no time for discussion. They want you there at eleven-fifteen."

"Where?"

"Hotel Wellington. Madison and Fifty-first. Room 1127."

"*Ben Hur?*"

"Elliot, get going, will you?"

"How did they hear of me?"

"I guess from 'A Brighter Tomorrow.' Or maybe they saw the thing about the whale."

"Nobody saw the thing about the whale. What does Morrie say about it?"

"He hasn't come in yet. They just called. Listen, Elliot, don't you want this thing?"

"Want it? Of course I want it."

"Then get going, will you?"

The enormity of my good fortune suddenly struck me.

"You bet!" I cried. "Teresa, you're fantastic. I love you!"

"Yeah, so I observed." Her voice turned shy. "Listen, as long as you love me, how about going out with me tomorrow night?"

"Tomorrow night?"

"Yeah. Billy Joel is at the Westbury Music Fair. You know where that is?"

"Out on Long Island someplace, I think."

"Yeah. Just about a half-hour from where I live. Morrie got me a pair of comps, and I don't have anybody to go with. Nobody special, I mean. So I thought maybe . . ."

"Sounds great."

"What?" She sounded surprised.

"I said it sounds great."

"You mean you don't have to go up to Rhode Island for your parents' wedding anniversary?"

"No. What gave you that idea?"

"That's what you told me last month when I had tickets for Paul Anka."

"Oh."

"Also the month before when I asked you to take me to my sister Anna's wedding."

"Oh. Well, uh, my folks were actually married twice. I mean, uh, well, it's a long story."

"Oh, that's okay. You don't have to explain. Listen, I live right on the way to the Music Fair, so why don't you come over for dinner first?"

"Oh, er, sure. Why not? I mean, er, sounds great."

I pictured her brothers as a band of apprentice Muzios and wondered if they served fish heads in slime.

"My mother usually makes cannelloni on Friday night. Her own homemade pasta."

"Can't beat that."

"You have to take a subway, then a bus," she said apologetically. "But after you get there we can borrow my brother Angelo's car to go to the concert."

"Fine."

She gave me directions. "About six-thirty, okay?"

"Sure." I glanced at the clock. It read ten forty-five. "I better get off the phone or else I'll never make it in time."

"Oh, God, yes. Good luck, Elliot."

"Thanks, Teresa."

It took me exactly seventeen minutes to shower, shave, and dress. Three of those minutes were lost in trying to determine what style of clothing best became a charioteer, a pair of L. L. Bean chinos and a dark blue sports shirt winning by default. I also lost two minutes calling Jerry's number and letting the phone ring fifteen times.

I thought of taking a taxi uptown, but a check of my wallet showed I was down to three dollars and fifty-six cents. It wasn't until I had locked the door behind me that I remembered the attaché case with four thousand dollars stashed under the bed. I ran back into the apartment, grabbed a couple of hundred dollars, returned the case to its hiding place, then hightailed it to the street where I caught a cab.

Who says that crime doesn't pay?

The Hotel Wellington on Madison Avenue is just about everything the Hotel Clayton on West Forty-eighth Street is not. Thick carpeting, brocaded sofas in the lobby, desk clerks who look like Alistair Cooke. The sound of a string quartet floated out of the restaurant and over the heads of the dignified, conservatively dressed patrons in the lobby. I thought I saw Catherine Deneuve step out of one of the elevators, but, as I was already five minutes late, I only had time for a quick stare.

I knocked at the door of room 1127 in a manner I hoped would sound confident without being overly brash. The knock of a disciplined man, stern and manly; just the sort you want to lead your Roman legions.

"Who is it?" A male voice, rather cultured, I thought.

"Elliot Fenway."

"Ah, yes. Come in."

The door opened and I stepped inside. On the other side of the room, with his back to the window, stood a man of sixty-odd years. About six feet tall and overweight, with thick, curly grey hair, bushy eyebrows and a very pale complexion. He gave me a sour, dyspeptic look.

Behind me the door closed and the lock turned

shut. Turning around, I saw a man of about thirty-five, slim and handsome with a lean, sensitive face and jet-black hair.

Both men were in shirtsleeves. Both were wearing shoulder holsters.

"Oh, shit!" I exclaimed. "Not again."

The younger man smiled at me.

"This time it's different," he said. "We're the good guys."

9

"I'm Inspector Baily of the New York Police Department," said the older man. He pointed to his companion. "This is Agent Bonello of the Federal Bureau of Investigation."

Once bitten, twice shy. "I suppose you guys have some identification," I said.

Without speaking or changing his slightly sour expression, the one called Baily reached into his hip pocket and brought out a small leather case. He held it open to reveal a badge and an ID card. I moved a little closer and examined it. As far as I could tell it was legitimate. Picture, signature, seal, plastic laminate, the works. After a few seconds I backed away. Baily's breath smelled of cheap cigars.

The other man also displayed an ID card, but I didn't bother to inspect it.

"Does this mean there's no Appian Productions?"

"I'm afraid not," said the younger man, smiling apologetically.

"No remake of *Ben Hur*, then, I suppose?"

"*Sic transit gloria,*" he said.

"Agent Bonello is a college man," said the dyspeptic-looking Baily. "Appian Productions was his idea."

"I was a classics major," explained the other.

I collapsed dolefully into an imitation Louis XV armchair.

"I probably wouldn't have gotten the part anyway."

"I'm sorry about the deception," said Bonello. "We thought it would be safer this way."

"Safer?"

"We didn't want the boys to know we were in touch with you."

"The boys? What boys? What are you talking about?"

"Come, come, Elliot." Baily's tone was as sour as his look. "You know what boys we're talking about. Your friends from Tozzi's."

He took out a package of antacid pills and popped one in his mouth.

"We think they're keeping an eye on you," explained Bonello. "They may even have put a bug in your apartment."

"A bug in my apartment?"

"Last night, while you were at the restaurant."

"But why?"

"They've lost the girl," he said. "Roxanne. They're waiting for her to get in touch with you, hoping you'll lead them to her."

"I don't understand this. How do you guys know I was at Tozzi's restaurant?"

"We have that place bugged," answered Baily. "Why should they be the only ones to listen in on conversations?"

"You mean you heard everything that went on last night?"

"Sure. We even have a recording of their recording of you taking the contract to kill John Barany. You want to hear it?"

"No."

He wagged a finger at me. "You've been a naughty boy, Elliot." He curled his mouth into a sour half-smile. "What are they handing out for fraud these days, Tony?"

"It's a little out of my line, Walt," answered the FBI man. "But I would imagine a year or two."

"Oh, at least." Baily unwrapped another antacid tablet. "Of course, it's not in my line, either. Really a case for the Bunco Division. My duty is just to report it to them." He chewed thoughtfully on the tablet. "Which I may or may not do, depending on you, Elliot."

"On me?"

"That's right. To tell you the truth I don't have much interest in seeing a young fellow locked up for a couple of years in a rat-hole where he'll just be abused and sodomized. Even if he is a two-bit ham actor trying to hustle a few bucks. What the hell, everybody's gotta live. Right, Tony?"

Bonello smiled. "You were always a compassionate guy, Walt."

Baily nodded. "What I am interested in is nailing Frank Tarabola. Now there's a guy worth locking up." He gave me an acidic smile. "Did you know, by the way, that Frank almost had you killed last night? There was a discussion about it after you left. You want to hear it?"

I felt a knot in my intestines.

"They were going to kill me?"

"They were thinking about it. They had their boy Vinnie call them to find out the decision. You may remember he stopped at a phone booth just before you left Brooklyn. On Tillary Street, right by the Post Office."

I stared at him dumbly. He smiled back sourly.

"How do you know where we stopped?" I asked.

"I was a block behind you," he replied.

Vinnie had indeed stopped to use a pay phone shortly before driving onto the bridge. Muzio had stayed with me in the back seat of the car. Now, as I tried to reconstruct the scene, I thought I recalled a quick exchange of glances between the two hoods and a slight shake of Vinnie's head when he returned from the phone booth. The recollection made me shudder.

"Incidentally, it's Nero you have to thank for being alive. He convinced the others you're more valuable to them that way. At least for the time being."

The room felt chillier; the temperature must have dropped several degrees.

"What's going on?" I asked. "What do those people want with me?"

"Let me tell you who they are first." Bonello spoke with quiet authority. "So you'll understand why it's important that we put them where they can't do any more harm. Also so that you will appreciate the need for caution. I'll start with Eraldo Giusti."

"Agent Bonello is the world's leading expert on Eraldo Giusti," Baily informed me, a note of admiration in his voice. "It was his number-one assignment when he was with the New York office, but since his promotion to Washington he only works part-time at it."

Bonello had taken a briefcase from the bed and pulled out a sheaf of eight-by-ten photographs. He showed me the top one, a studio portrait of the white-haired Don with the marble complexion.

"This is Eraldo Giusti," he said. "Came to the U.S.

at the age of two; joined the Luciano mob at nineteen. That was in 1931. In 1937 he fled the country, charged with murdering three men in a Brooklyn restaurant. For the next eight years he lived in Italy, where he ingratiated himself with the Fascist government by arranging the murder of two enemies of Mussolini who ran an Italian-language newspaper in New York. In the middle of the war, when the tide was turning, he switched sides and made himself very useful to Allied intelligence; so useful that all previous charges against him back in the U.S. were dropped. He returned home just in time for a bloody series of gang wars and emerged as one of the leaders of the New York underworld. Known to be directly or indirectly responsible for the deaths of seventeen people, but never served a single day in prison. Currently in retirement and sliding into senility, but trotted out from time to time when an elder statesman figurehead is required."

"Sort of like Richard Nixon," I ventured. Neither man laughed.

"Frank Tarabola," Bonello continued, "started serving under Don Giusti in 1948, specializing in the garrote. You know what that is? A length of wire with a wooden handle on each end, used for strangling. Two men work it, one on each handle, with the victim wrapped up in the middle."

Baily took up the narrative, pointing to a picture of Tarabola in a tuxedo with his arms around the shoulders of Enginehead and the man with the toupee. All three smiled broadly out of the photograph at me.

"Frank's partner in those early days was Louie Cavallo, known as Louie the Horse. You dined with him last night at Tozzi's. The garrote, by the way, is not a weapon for the fastidious, since one of its side effects is the voiding of the victim's bladder, but there is no record of that ever bothering Frank or Louie. When less aromatic methods were desired there was always Willie 'The Rabbit' Coniglio, whom you also met last night. His specialty was the ice pick."

He favored me with one of his sour smiles as I shuddered.

"Young Michael Nero, on the other hand, having no training in the ice pick or garrote, found even nastier weapons. A law degree and an MBA. Williams College class of 1972, followed by Wharton for business and Notre Dame for law. In between Wharton and Notre Dame he married the daughter of Frank Tarabola. The Tarabolas and the Neros have family and business ties going all the way back to the old country."

"Nero is one of the new breed," said Bonello. "Smooth, well educated, ambitious."

"And dangerous," added Baily. "Full of ideas about cost accounting and risk analysis, but at heart as greedy and ruthless as any old-time mafioso."

"Sounds like most of the MBA's I've met," I said.

Baily grinned with pleasure. "Agent Bonello has an MBA."

"Nero is trying to bring the mob into the 1980s." Bonello spoke with perfect aplomb, ignoring the previous interchange. "They're really losing ground by following the old ways. Competition is too keen: South Americans cutting in on the drug trade, Oriental imports making big inroads in the prostitution market. The younger guys like Michael Nero see the handwriting on the wall unless they can keep costs down and increase productivity. A marriage of organized crime with high technology and modern business methods. But the old guard is hard to move."

I tried to imagine Muzio grappling with the LOTUS software package.

"What's this got to do with me?" I asked.

"Not much," Bonello admitted. "I just find it fascinating." He smiled coolly. "One MBA observing another, I suppose."

"All right, Elliot," said Baily. "Let's get to you. You were hired to ice John Barany. John the Baron, known as Janos when he came to this country in 1956. Fresh from the uprising in Hungary, supposedly one of the freedom fighters. Got a job as a waiter in a restaurant owned by Frank Tarabola's brother and worked his way to he top by seducing the boss's daughter. He was close to thirty at the time; she was seventeen. They were married in what used to be called a shotgun wedding. In other words, she was pregnant and Janos was persuaded to make her an honest woman. As it turned out she lost the baby, but by that time our Johnny was a member of one of New York's most prominent families. Prominent, at least, in extortion, prostitution, and hijacking circles."

He took another antacid pill and chewed it as he spoke.

"Janos Barany prospered in this country. Made a bundle, in fact. High-toned restaurant and a string of fancy delicatessens, not to mention one of the biggest distributorships of speciality frozen foods on the East Coast. All thanks to his in-laws, who he gratefully paid back in services rendered. Laundering money, mostly. A lot of money. Last year alone he must have handled over a couple of million for them."

I started to interrupt with a question, but he held up his hand.

"Let me finish," he said. "Lately the accounts have been coming up short. There seem to be discrepancies in the books, more dirty money coming in than clean money going out. Young Nero was the first to discover it. As far as we know there's a couple of hundred thousand unaccounted for, and its got the boys chewing the furniture."

"It doesn't sound like a big enough amount to get them all that upset," I ventured. Baily snorted.

"I don't know where you hang out, but in the part of Queens where I live it's considered a tidy sum."

"I just meant in a, er, business like that, where they're dealing in millions . . ."

"You don't know the minds of people like that. Those guys can't bear to see a penny slip out of their grasp. A man like Tarabola would feed his brother to the sharks for welching on a ten-dollar World Series bet. Besides, they're worried that it may only be the tip of the iceberg. Nero has spent the last few weeks going over the accounts, trying to figure out how long the bucket has been leaking."

He took out a cigar. "Do you mind if I smoke?" he asked, curling his lip around it and lighting up without waiting for an answer.

"There are several suspects," he explained through a cloud of smoke. "The main one is Roxanne Adair, your friend from the Hotel Clayton, an ex-stripper and high-class whore who Barany keeps on his payroll. She calls herself an actress, but her dramatic appearances seem to be limited to faking orgasms for rich old men. Which is not the only reason the Baron keeps her on retainer. She also rides herd on Tarabola's stable of hookers and acts as bag lady, collecting large amounts of money from the street and delivering it to the Budapest laundry service. Only not all of it gets delivered, apparently."

"Buy why does she want to have Barany killed?" I asked.

"Well," replied Baily, "now you've asked the sixty-four-thousand-dollar question. That's just what the Tarabola mob wants to know and so do we. Nero holds to the view that Barany and Roxanne are working together to swindle the company, in which case she might want him out of the way so she doesn't have to share the wealth. Or maybe she was working alone and Barany got wise and has been shaking her down. But whatever it is, Nero is convinced Roxanne is the key to the missing money, and that she'll lead them to whoever else is involved. That's why he's had her watched for the last week or so."

He took a long puff of cigar smoke and exhaled it in my direction.

"And now they're counting on you, Mr. Fenway Park, to lead them to Roxanne. Is that your real name, by the way?"

"Why? What has that got to do with any of this?"

"Nothing. Just curious."

"Well, as a matter of fact it isn't. My real name is Feinstein. Elliot Feinstein. Fenway is just the name I use in my career as two-bit ham actor."

He looked pleased with himself.

"Okay, Mr. Feinstein Park, that's it. You play ball with us and maybe we can forget about your little cameo role as Son of Murder Incorporated."

"What am I supposed to do?"

"That depends on what happens. Right now you

just wait to hear from the girl. Just go about your normal routine—ballet classes, diction lessons, unemployment line, whatever—until she gets in touch with you. If and when that occurs we may want you to meet her. We'll have to see what happens."

"She already got in touch with me," I said.

"What?"

I told them about Roxanne's call of the previous afternoon.

"Did you tell Tarabola or any of the others about it?"

"No. I was holding it in reserve as a useful tidbit in case I needed it, but it never came to that."

"You're sure you didn't mention it to Vinnie during the car ride?"

"I'm positive."

Baily and Bonello looked at each other.

"I don't see how that changes anything," said the older man.

"No," agreed his younger colleague. "If anything, it makes it more likely she'll be back in touch."

Baily wrote two phone numbers on the back of a business card and handed it to me.

"Here. I can be reached at either of these numbers. Call me as soon as you hear from her. If I'm out, leave a number where I can call you back."

"Will I be in much danger?" I asked.

He smiled crookedly. "Clint Eastwood wouldn't think twice about it."

"I don't think you'll be much at risk," Bonello said.

I looked around the posh hotel room with its heavy gold drapes, deep-pile carpeting, and brand-new antique furniture.

"Did you guys rent this room just to talk to me? It must have cost a bundle."

"It's my room," Bonello replied. "I checked in last night from Washington."

"The FBI must give you guys one hell of a per diem allowance," I said. "Makes me kind of glad I didn't earn enough to pay taxes last year."

Bonello stiffened. "The Bureau allows forty dollars a day. I make up the rest myself."

"Agent Bonello has what they call an independent income," Baily explained in an amused tone. "He doesn't have to work for a living the way poor slobs like me do. Or defraud helpless women the way poor slobs like you do."

"I'm sorry I asked," I said.

I looked down, fixing my gaze on Agent Bonello's Gucci loafers.

"Well, Elliot, what about it?" asked Baily. "Are you going to help us?"

"Do I have any choice?" I asked unhappily.

"You could always do one-to-three for fraud and larceny."

I looked up at them.

"What the hell," I said. "I might as well work for you guys. You're the first ones in ten months to offer me a part."

"Good." Baily nodded. "Now so far we've been doing most of the talking. It's time you told us a few things."

"Like what?" I asked.

"Why don't you start by telling us how you got hooked up with Roxanne."

"I met her in a bar."

"Yeah, that's what you told the boys at Tozzi's. It wasn't very convincing."

"What do you mean?"

"What bar?"

"I don't remember the name."

"She was just there by herself?"

"Yes."

"How'd the subject come up?"

"I don't know, we just started talking."

"I see. Just a little casual conversation. The weather, baseball, whatever. And then she comes out and asks you to kill somebody."

"Well, no. Not exactly."

"What then, exactly?"

"Well, we sort of started talking, then I, er . . ."

There was a silence. Bonello looked soberly at me.

"You're not going to help yourself by lying to us," he said.

"A friend of mine set it up," I admitted.

Baily was immediately alert. "What friend? Who is he?"

"Do I have to tell you that? I don't really want to get anyone else in trouble."

"That's noble of you, really noble. You're the noblest asshole I ever met."

"Your friend didn't seem too concerned about getting you into trouble," added Bonello.

"Well, I know, but . . ."

"Who is he?" Baily insisted. "Another actor?"

"Not exactly. He's a nightclub comic."

The two men looked at each other. Bonello raised an eyebrow slightly. Baily shook his head and chuckled mirthlessly.

"I'd rather not give his name," I added.

"You don't have to give his name." Baily gave me a derisive glance, then turned back to his colleague. "You called the shot on that one."

"What are you talking about?" I asked.

"We know him. His name is Jerry De Marco."

I gaped at him. "How do you know that?"

"He's up to his ears in it. He does a lot of odd jobs for the mob. Bag man, pusher, a little pimping. He's on Nero's list of suspects, as a matter of fact, but they don't really think he has the nerve to steal from them."

"They could have been in it together," Bonello said thoughtfully. "They used to be lovers, after all."

"Jerry and Roxanne?" I asked.

Bonello nodded. "That's right. Before he took up with Marie Barany."

I thought with sadness of Gloria.

"Are you sure he's mixed up in this?"

"Look for yourself," said Bonello. He shuffled through the pile of photographs and handed several to me. "These were taken last year at Frank Tarabola's sixty-fifth birthday party."

There was one of Jerry dancing with a tall, svelte, fortyish woman with short dark hair.

"That's Marie Barany," Baily informed me. "According to gossip, she and Jerry haven't confined their activities to dancing."

He pointed to another photo.

"There's the Baron himself."

Jerry and Barany stood on either side of a flashy, tough-looking blonde in her early thirties. Their arms were draped around her shoulders and they smiled broadly at her as she stuck her tongue out at the camera.

"Who's the blonde?" I asked.

Baily gave me a look of surprise.

"You don't know?" he asked.

"No. Am I supposed to?"

He and Bonello exchanged puzzled glances.

"This may be more complicated than we thought," he said. "That's Roxanne Adair."

10

I called Jerry from a phone booth in the lobby. He wasn't in.

"He didn't come home last night," Gloria told me in a downcast voice. "It happens a lot lately. To tell you the truth, Elliot, I think he's having an affair."

She thought he was having an affair. It was like saying Imelda Marcos owned some shoes.

"I'm sorry to hear that," I replied. It sounded pretty feeble, but I didn't know what else to say.

"Look, Elliot, do you think you could come up here for a while? I could use somebody to talk to."

"You mean right now?" I asked.

"I could make something for lunch. You haven't eaten yet, have you?"

"Well no, but . . ."

"It's just that I'm feeling a little shaky and thought it might help to have some company, you know?"

Her speech was a little slurred. I wondered if she had been drinking.

"I mean, I don't want to impose or anything. Just if you don't have anything else to do."

Ten years ago I thought I had loved her. It was hard to turn her down.

"No, no. Nothing important," I assured her. "I'll come right over."

She showed no signs of intoxication when she let

me into the apartment. No alcohol on her breath, no stagger in her walk. Just a brittleness of manner, a fluttering of her hands, an excess of lipstick smeared on her mouth that was very unlike the Gloria I knew. She came to the door wearing a pair of cork wedgies and a wraparound flowery cotton print thing that was either a housedress or else the latest fashion in New York at-home wear.

"Thanks for coming." She brushed her lips against me and gave me a little hug.

"What are friends for?"

I stiffened a bit in her embrace, caught between an urge to hug her back and an impulse to wriggle free. Her skin was warm and soft and smelled of perfumed soap. She must have recently showered, for the ends of her short brown hair were wet. She roused desires in me I thought had died years before.

"Come on in. Let's visit a spell before lunch." She led me by the hand into the living room. "I'm playing hooky from the bank today, and I have the most wonderful recipe for chicken-and-pear salad with chutney sauce. I'm dying to try it out on someone who'll appreciate it."

She threw herself onto an immense white couch and motioned me to sit beside her.

"Oh, it's good to see you, Elliot. What's new with you?"

What was new with me? I made a mental list. Since yesterday I had taken a contract for murder, been abducted by a band of gangsters, and had just come from a forty-five-minute session with an FBI agent and a detective who had coerced me into assisting them.

"Nothing much," I answered. "How about you?"

She sighed.

"Well, my marriage is on the rocks, I've been drinking too much, and I think I'm on the verge of a nervous breakdown. How's that for openers?"

I ruled it a draw between us.

"I'm sorry to hear about you and Jerry," I said. "You really think it's beyond repair?"

She gave a soft, mirthless laugh.

"I think it was beyond repair when it was new. I just didn't know it then. Christ, the things I've closed my eyes to over the years, hoping they'd go away."

She dropped her pitch and exaggerated her drawl.

"Believe me, podner, I could unfold a tale whose lightest word would . . . would what? What's the line?"

" 'Whose lightest word would harrow up thy soul, freeze thy young blood.' "

She smiled. "I knew you'd know it."

I shrugged modestly. "I think I know every part in *Hamlet* by heart."

"Even Ophelia?"

" 'There's rosemary,' " I quoted, " 'that's for remembrance; pray love, remember; and there is pansies, that's for thoughts.' "

We stared at each other in silence. I felt a great tenderness toward her.

"Oh Elliot," she sighed, "why the hell didn't I fall in love with you way back when I had the chance?"

"I don't know. I was sure stuck on you at the time."

"Were you? You certainly didn't show it. Why didn't you say something, make some move?"

"Shy, I guess. A little afraid." I shrugged. "I never

was a very fast worker, and by the time I got up the nerve you were already, er . . ."

I made a vague gesture of hopelessness.

"Carrying another man's child. Is that what you're trying to say?" She smiled. "Thanks for trying to find a delicate way to put it, but I just got myself plain old knocked up."

"Yeah, well it did kind of put a crimp in my plans."

"Put a crimp in *your* plans? Hey, I was going to be the next Uta Hagen, remember? Play Saint Joan, Desdemona, Blanche Dubois. Take Broadway by storm. Remember how good I was as Cleopatra?"

"How could I forget? We were doing that scene when you told me."

"Told you? Oh my God." She clapped her hands together and broke into a laugh. "Oh my God, how could I forget that? The look on your face. Right in front of the whole acting class."

I nodded, unsmiling. It was a trip down Memory Lane I could have done without, having made it enough times on my own.

"You were in the middle of your death scene," she went on, "with your head in my lap, and I was sort of bending over you like this."

She pulled me toward her until I was lying on the couch, my head resting on her thigh.

"Uh, Gloria . . ."

"What was your line? Say your line." She leaned over me and placed a hand on my forehead.

" 'I am dying, Egypt, dying.' "

"And I am pregnant, Feinstein, pregnant," she said in a heavy whisper. "O God, Elliot, do you remember?"

"Yes, I remember."

She started to laugh, but let it die away quickly.

"Oh Christ. I was so stupid."

"You could have at least called me Fenway."

There were tears in her eyes. I reached up and touched her face, then drew her down to me and kissed her. A long, involved kiss. Her mouth tasted slightly of whiskey. "I'm sorry, Gloria." I sat up and moved away from her. "I shouldn't have done that."

She smiled shyly. "It sure felt good."

I resisted an urge to kiss her again.

"I mean under the circumstances it just doesn't seem . . . Oh God, I don't know . . . honorable, I guess. Of me, I mean. Under the circumstances."

Her smile broadened.

"Don't make such a big thing of it, Elliot. It's just something that happened. I know you're an honorable person, the most honorable I know. I've always admired you for that."

That's what you think, I thought. Talk about unfolding a tale.

"Just a case of bad timing," I said.

"Sure," she agreed.

"Maybe some day, if you and Jerry really do break up . . . if I haven't had anything to do with it, I mean . . . I mean maybe . . . well, of course, I have a few problems of my own to straighten out. But maybe someday . . ."

"I'm thinking of going back to Montana," she said abruptly. "For good, I mean. I'm sick of it all. Sick of New York, sick of all this." She made a gesture that took in the apartment and its furnishings, all the glass and tubular steel and dazzling white upholstery. "I want to go back where I can ride horses and breathe fresh air. Did you know that when I was a kid I was a great outdoorsman?"

"Yes. You used to talk about it a lot when you first came to New York."

"Life was so good back there, so clean and simple. I sometimes wonder why I ever left. Have you ever slept under the open sky, Elliot?"

"Yes. When I was in high school back in Rhode Island my cousin Melvin and I used to camp out on the beach all the time."

"Was it wonderful?"

"Yes, it was. A sky full of stars, the sound of the surf, the smell of salt air. I never tasted anything like the fish we used to broil over an open fire out there."

"Don't you ever get the urge to go back to it? Just kick everything over and get out? Leave New York, with its noise and crowds and gritty dirt and slimy hustlers, get away from the daily humiliations, the hassle, the aggression, and just go where you can breathe clean air?"

I waited a few beats before making the obvious response.

"What, and give up show business?"

She gave forth a healthy burst of laughter.

"Come on, Feinstein. Let's have lunch."

Lunch was cheerful enough. The chicken-and-pear salad was a great success and we washed it down with a large quantity of Pouilly-Fuissé. Over two bottles I think it was, though in truth my recollection is a bit fuzzy, for the wine divided about three to one in my favor. By the time we said good-bye a sweet giddiness had overtaken me and my inhibitions had melted away. This time it was she who backed off.

"Thanks for coming, Elliot. It really helped a lot."

I made a courtly bow and lost my balance.

" 'Lady,' " I said, putting a hand on her shoulder to steady myself, " 'by yonder blessed moon I swear, That tips with silver all these fruit-tree tops—' "

" 'O!' " she responded, " 'swear not by the moon, the inconstant moon, that monthly changes in her' something, something, 'lest that thy love prove' something, something else."

She smiled a little sadly.

"Sorry, Elliot, I can't remember it. It's been a long time."

"Sure."

I bobbed my head a little, feeling dizzy.

"Listen, Gloria, about you and Jerry. If there's anything I can do . . . I mean, if you need somebody to talk to . . ."

She brushed my cheek lightly with her lips and gave me the briefest of hugs.

"Thanks," she said. "You're a real pal. Whatever happens I want you to know I really care for you. A lot."

I leaned over to kiss her again, but she slipped beneath my arm.

"I think you'd better go now before we get carried away and do something foolish."

"Sure," I concurred. It dawned on me I might be a little drunk.

"Don't forget," she called after me as I lurched toward the elevator, "I really care about what happens to you. So take care of yourself, huh?"

"You bet," I assured her as the elevator door closed behind me.

By the time I hit street level I was in the grip of a delicious, tipsy melancholy. A sweet, sad sense of longing for . . . for whom? For Gloria, of course. Or was it for Roxanne? Or Maud? Or maybe even for Lisa Duncan, whose lesbian lover had deserted her for a fashion model, and whose baby (and mine) was at that very moment being held hostage by her temporarily deranged ex-husband. Everyone, it seemed, had a share of woe.

I walked to Broadway and hailed a taxi. The sun was strong, the air still, and the heat rose in waves from the sidewalk and made me feel even dizzier.

"Where to?" asked the driver as I climbed into the rear of the cab.

"Who cares?" I asked in reply. " 'I hold the world but as the world, Gratiano; a stage where every man must play a part, and mine a sad one.' "

"Okay by me," he said agreeably. "Just tell me where you want to play it."

" 'All the world's a stage,' " I explained, " 'and all the men and women merely players: They have their exits and their entrances.' "

"I don't know from all the world," he said. "I only work Manhattan."

"In that case make it Mercer Street. Number 180."

"One-eighty Mercer Street it is. And the name ain't Graziano, it's Vuckovic."

Following that exchange I must have dozed, for the next thing I was aware of was Vuckovic reaching over the back of his seat and shaking my knee.

"Hey, Hamlet, we're here. One-eighty Mercer Street. Exit, door left."

"Huh? Oh. That was fast."

I climbed out of the cab and dug in my pockets for the rest of the money I had taken that morning. There was a twenty and a couple of small bills.

"Keep the change," I said, handing him the twenty.

"Okay, thanks," he replied. "You gonna be all right?"

"Just fine," I assured him.

"Good luck, then. I hope you get the part."

He ground gears and took off. I looked around for any Muzios who might be lurking in the shadows but saw nobody suspicious. A few run-of-the-mill vagrants, to be sure, and one or two characters with whom I would not want to share a dark alley, but nobody who looked like they played with garrotes.

The mellowness of half an hour earlier had dissipated and, instead of a warm glow, had left a dull ache in my temples. My stomach felt like a small boat in a very choppy sea, and my hands shook as I unlocked the door. What I saw when I opened it did not make me feel any steadier.

The place had been ransacked, vandalized, turned upside down. Couch and chairs turned over, cushions scattered, upholstery slashed. The door had been torn off the little commode; the mirror above it smashed. The little Chinese vase that Phil swore was genuine Ching dynasty lay in shards on the floor. Books were lying everywhere. It was hard to walk without stepping on them.

My knees began to wobble, my head was reeling, and my stomach sent shudders of distress throughout my digestive system. I tried to tiptoe around the wreckage and get to the bathroom, but midway across my legs gave out. I sank to the floor and threw up on the carpet.

11

After a while, after I had run out of bits of chicken-and-pear salad in chutney sauce to bring up, I got to my feet and looked around the room. It was the greatest scene of devastation I had witnessed since the last act of *Hamlet*.

Somehow I managed to make it to the bathroom without breaking or tripping over anything on the floor. I washed my face and rinsed my mouth in an effort to get rid of the taste of chutney mixed with bile.

Back in the living room the phone was ringing. I walked to where it sat on a small end table that had somehow managed to remain standing amid the rubble.

"Help," I said into the mouthpiece as I sank onto a shredded couch cushion.

"Elliot, is that you? This is Phil."

"Phil?"

"Yeah, Phil. Phil Bender. You know, your, er, landlord."

He laughed as though he had just said something funny, then suddenly cut it off.

"Hey, did you just say 'help'?"

My head felt a little clearer. The dizziness seemed to be passing.

"No, I meant hello. That is, I *said* hello. It must have sounded like help."

"Oh dear, did I wake you up? What time is it there? I thought it was afternoon."

I looked around for a clock.

"It's noon here," he went on without waiting for an answer. "I've been up since five, can you believe it? Things really start early out here. Don't let anybody hand you that line about California being laid back. They work your tail off."

His jauntiness heightened my sense of doom.

"Anyway, I'm sorry if I woke you. I just wanted to tell you I'm coming home sooner than expected."

"Coming home?"

"Yes. I finished the first phase of the job about a month ahead of schedule and the rest of the production is bogged down, so there's no point in my hanging around. In fact, I can probably do all the rest of the work in New York with only a few short trips back here."

"You're coming home? To New York?"

"That's right. I can't say I'll be all that sorry to leave California. To tell you the truth—"

"You mean here? To this apartment?"

"Yes, of course, where else? It's where I live, isn't it? Elliot, what's the matter with you?"

I didn't reply. My stomach had just received the news and was not digesting it well.

"Oh, I get it," exclaimed Phil brightly. "I see what's bothering you."

"Uh, Phil, I don't think you can really see what's bothering me."

"Of course I can. You're worried about not having a place to live. I should have set your mind at rest about that right off."

"Uh, Phil, that's not my main problem right now."

"Listen, Elliot." He spoke on top of my words. "There's nothing to worry about. You're more than welcome to stay until you find some digs of your own. The couch is really very comfortable."

I looked at the overturned couch, big chunks of foam rubber protruding from the tears in its velvet covering. I decided not to tell Phil it was not as comfortable as he remembered.

"When are you getting back?" I asked.

"Tuesday night."

"Tuesday night?" I had expected something vague and distant like the middle of next month. "What day is today?"

"What day is today?" he echoed, adding a little chuckle. "Boy, you're really out of it, aren't you? Today is Thursday."

"Thursday! And you're coming home on Tuesday?"

"That's right." He chuckled again. "I guess you'll have to clean the place up in a hurry."

I looked at the commode with its doors torn off and its mirror smashed, then past the Ching dynasty fragments to the puddle of bile and chicken salad on the carpet.

"No problem," I told him.

By the time I hung up my stomach had started sending me nasty messages again. I went back into the bathroom and stood retching over the sink. It was mostly a case of dry convulsions, my harrowed-up soul having already been by and large deposited on the living-room rug. I once again washed my mouth out, grabbed a bottle of Pepto-Bismol from the top shelf of the medicine cabinet, and downed about half a pint while trying to figure out my next move.

"Call the cops," said the left side of my brain. "Flee to Costa Rica," said the right. After a brief debate the left prevailed. My passport was out of date.

I was on my way back to the phone when it started to ring.

"Phil? It's me, Roxanne."

I did not reply.

"What'd you decide?"

"Decide?"

"About my money. Do I get it back?"

I looked around at the shambles of Phil Bender's apartment. A sense of outrage, a gush of warm anger rose from the pit of my stomach. Anger at Jerry, at Muzio and Vinnie, at Tarabola, at Baily, at everyone who had been threatening and browbeating and deceiving me lately. But mostly at her, because she was closest to hand, I suppose. Or maybe because she was the only one I felt capable of taking on if push came to shove.

"Yes," I said quietly. "You can have your money back. I don't want any trouble."

"That's wise, Phil."

"How do we get together?"

"There's a place called Dante's Paradise on Columbus Avenue between Sixty-fifth and Sixty-sixth. How about meeting me there in about an hour?"

"Fine," I said.

"I'll be in one of the back booths, as far back as I can."

"I can't wait."

After she hung up I thought briefly about calling Bonello but rejected the idea. It would be better to find out what she was up to before deciding whether to bring in the cops. That way I might still have a chance of hanging on to my fair share of the hit money. And once my anger ebbed a bit I remembered how damned attractive she was. Why introduce her to a handsome FBI man in a Brooks Brothers blazer?

Besides, I didn't think I needed help on this one. She certainly didn't strike me as dangerous. All the same I decided to take along the unloaded pistol in case I had to scare her away, plus a few hundred dollars in case I had to buy her off.

The bedroom was in the same shape as the living room. Mattress slashed open, pillows ripped apart, dresser drawers emptied of their contents and thrown on the floor. I reached under the bed for the attaché case containing the .22 and the cash. It was gone.

Dante's Paradise turned out to be a gourmet fast-food joint, long and narrow, with a counter running down one side and about twenty booths down the other. Roxanne, or whoever she was, was in the next-to-last. She looked breathtaking in a charcoal-grey jump suit, her blonde hair tied back to show off a pair of long jade earrings.

"I'm glad you came, Phil. You're doing the right thing."

I slid into the booth and grabbed her wrist.

"Who are you?" I demanded roughly.

"Hey! Let go of my wrist."

"Who are you?" I repeated.

She pulled her arm from my grasp but I grabbed it again. We tugged back and forth across the table.

"Let go of me, damn you!"

"I want to know who you are and what your game is."

"I already told you who I am. Roxanne."

"Don't give me that. I know you're not Roxanne Adair."

"Well, for that matter, I know you're not Phil Bender."

"What?"

"Now let go of my arm or I'm going to scream."

"How do you know I'm not Phil Bender?"

She opened her mouth and started to throw her head back. I hastily released her. Looking quickly around I saw a stocky, broad-shouldered waiter staring at us.

"Women!" I sneered loudly, rolling my eyes. Then I leaned forward and spoke softly to the blonde. "Please tell me who you are."

She sat there rubbing her wrist, looking sullen.

"I thought you were a nice guy," she said. "A sensitive person."

"I didn't mean to hurt you."

"Oh, I'll bet."

"It's just that I have to find out what's going on. Tarabola and those guys don't fool around. You should see what they did to my apartment."

"Who's Tarabola?"

"Are you kidding? You don't know who Tarabola is?"

She shook her head.

"Michael Nero?"

"I never heard of him."

"Well, they're gangsters. You may be in a lot of trouble."

She looked scared. "I knew I shouldn't get mixed

up in it," she said, dropping her glance. "I wouldn't have done it if I didn't have a lot of debts."

"Done what?"

"Pretended to be Roxanne."

"You mean you were paid to do it?"

She nodded unhappily.

"You got paid to set me up? Why?"

"It was nothing personal," she said. "Just a part."

"Just a part? What do you mean, just a part? You led me to believe you were someone else. You took money to do it. What kind of person are you?"

She drew herself up in her seat.

"I'm an actress," she said with dignity.

"It started with this friend of mine," she explained a few minutes later, after the waiter had taken our order. "Sort of an ex-boyfriend, I guess you'd say. I used to go out with him until I found out he was married. Anyway, he came to see me about a week ago with an undercover policeman."

"An undercover policeman?"

"Yes. He said he wanted to hire me to play the part of someone wanting to hire a hit man. Said it was part of an investigation he was working on."

"And you believed him?" I asked incredulously.

"Why shouldn't I have believed him?"

"Because undercover cops don't hire actresses to help them with their investigations. Did you ask to see any identification?"

"I told you he was with a friend of mine. They said he was an undercover agent for the New York Police Department investigating a murder-for-hire ring and he needed someone who wouldn't be recognized by the mob."

"What a flimsy story! Were you really dumb enough to believe that?"

She looked close to tears.

"I told you. I had a lot of debts."

"Ah, so you weren't dumb. Just greedy."

"You're not being very nice."

"Nice? Nice? How the hell do you expect me to be nice? The mob is after me; the FBI is leaning on me. My apartment has been demolished, and if I'm lucky I'll just go to jail instead of being buried in concrete. And all because you wanted to make a few bucks."

She thrust her lower lip forward and glared truculently at me.

"Well, what about you?" she asked. "You're not exactly an innocent victim, are you? What about the four thousand dollars I gave you? Who was setting who up? At least I didn't take any money from you."

"Ah . . . er . . . um," I explained.

"Exactly," she concurred. "So I don't think you're in any position to talk about being greedy." Her tone softened a bit. "Oh, I don't hold it against you. I know the kinds of things an actor has to do to survive. But you're hardly in a position to be judgmental."

I stared at her in surprise.

"You know I'm an actor?"

"Of course I know you're an actor. I knew it from the first time I saw you on Riverside Drive."

"How did you know?"

"I used to watch you on that soap opera."

" 'A Brighter Tomorrow'?"

"Yes."

"Oh."

I waited for her to say something more.

"What did you think of it?" I finally asked.

She smiled. "I thought you were terrific. The best one on the show."

"Not better than Dr. Todd Duncan," I said modestly.

"Much better," she insisted. "In fact, I stopped watching after they killed you off."

"No kidding!"

"I also saw you do Mercutio in that church down on the East Side."

"No kidding!" I repeated. "Not many people saw that one."

She didn't say how she liked that performance, but I was too shy to ask.

"My name is Elliot Fenway," I told her.

"I know," she replied. "Mine's Amanda Cole. It's really Kolacz, but I changed it when I came to New York."

"Mine's really Feinstein." I peered at her. "Now that I think of it I'm sure I've seen you before. What have you done?"

"Oh, God," she said shyly. "Nothing like you. I worked the office-equipment show at the Coliseum last winter. I was Miss Minolta Desk Copier."

"I didn't catch it," I said apologetically.

"I also worked as an extra once. *Prizzi's Honor.* I was one of the wedding guests."

"That's it! I knew I'd seen you before."

She shook her head. "I only danced by for a split second on the upper right-hand corner of the screen. Anyway, they cut it."

"It gets discouraging, doesn't it?"

"Sometimes. But I'm going to make it." She

sounded very determined. "What I really want to do is Broadway musicals. I'm a pretty good dancer."

"I'll bet you're great."

"I almost had a regular spot on TV, but it fell through. Actually, I'm glad it did. Who wants to go to California?"

"That's just how I feel."

"Especially to work for Binky Bannerman."

"Binky Bannerman?"

"You know, the host of 'Getting and Spending'? My agent had it all set up for me to be his assistant, but he gave the job to some actress he was sleeping with."

"Some actress he was sleeping with?"

She nodded. "For a couple of years, on and off, whenever he was in New York. Anyway, I'm glad it worked out the way it did. Especially after the things I've heard about his sexual practices."

We sat in silence for a minute or so. Then I reached across the table and took her hand.

"I'm sorry if I hurt your wrist," I said.

"No, it's okay. I guess I don't blame you for being upset."

I looked into her beautiful green eyes.

"I'm glad you didn't go to California," I said.

She smiled. It reminded me of how it felt when I was a kid and saw the sun come up over Narragansett Bay after a storm.

"Do you eat Chinese food in bed?" I asked.

"No, of course not. What kind of question is that?"

"Roxanne," I said tenderly.

"Amanda," she corrected me, smiling gently.

"Amanda," I murmured. "I think I love you."

12

Next day I slept till noon. When I awoke she was gone. On the kitchen counter there was a note.

Raven:
    I won't be back till 5. Lots and lots of things to do—dance class, photo session, etc., etc., etc.
    Mr. Coffee's all set up, just switch it on. All kinds of food in the fridge, just help yourself.
    See you tonight?

                                                        Rox
P.S. You were a hit, man!

I made a quick tour of the apartment while the Mr. Coffee did its business. Not a bad setup, I decided. The building, like the neighborhood, was old and run-down enough to give hope that the rent might still be in three figures. A three-flight climb up dingy stairways redolent of garbage and cat pee and cooked cabbage and a host of other smells that had probably seeped into the plaster some time during the Great Depression. Inside the apartment, however, all was cheerful and well maintained. A cute little kitchen the width of an ironing board, two bedrooms—one small, the other not quite that big—and a bathroom the size of the back seat of a Chevy Nova. But the living room was large and bright, with two big windows looking down on the street.

All in all a decent place for sharing, a place to cheer the heart of a young man about to be cast adrift in the shark-infested waters of Manhattan real estate.

Not that I am really as calculating as all that. Desperate though I was for housing I had strong misgivings about casting my lot with yet another actress, and would not have been ready to subject myself to the ups and downs of quasi-connubial life had I not been knocked head over heels by Amanda.

I had been swept away from the start, showing not a trace of my usual *sang froid*. She, on the other hand, had managed to retain a certain degree of hers.

We had walked from Dante's Paradise to her flat, a few blocks north and a long block west, arm in arm through the early city evening as the lights were beginning to come on. Just inside the entrance to her apartment, as we bumped against each other in the narrow little hallway, she let me draw her to me and kiss her, a long, serious kiss, full of mystery and promise.

"You're sweet," she said, leaning back against my arms. "You really are."

"I think I love you," I said.

"I know. You told me that in Dante's." She smiled. "Are your declarations of love always so definite?"

"Well, I, er . . ."

"Hush," she whispered, putting her hand against my mouth. She moved it along my chin and up against my cheek, then leaned toward me and kissed me again.

"God, you are sweet," she said dreamily, leaning lazily against me. "But . . ." She straightened up and cuffed me playfully on the chest a few times. "We had better not get too carried away too fast." She slipped out of my arms. "What do you say we have some coffee?"

She went to the sink and held a Mr. Coffee carafe under the tap. I moved behind her and put my hands on her shoulders.

"Amanda," I murmured into the nape of her neck. She smelled heavenly.

"Elliot!" She shook me off. "Calm down, will you?" She turned to face me, holding the carafe in one hand as she pushed me away with the other. She backed me down the narrow kitchen to the coffee maker.

"Look," she said, "I like you a lot; I really do. But don't rush things, okay? We have important things to discuss before we get too emotional."

I knew right away what she meant. I had dealt with actresses before.

"You're going to tell me you don't want to get involved with an actor, right? You're afraid of career conflicts, clashes of temperament. What a hackneyed viewpoint."

"That isn't what I had in mind," she said firmly. "Right now I'm more worried about things like gangsters and police and ransacked apartments and possible fraud charges."

"Oh."

She poured us each a cup of coffee and we went into the living room.

"We could both be in big trouble, don't you think? We ought to do something about that before we get too wrapped up in our personal relationship."

I saw her point.

"I suppose an important prerequisite to any deep personal relationship is that both parties stay out of jail," I conceded.

"Yes," she agreed. "And that at least one maintains an undemolished apartment."

"Uh, speaking of that, it will take all day to make mine habitable. You don't suppose I could, er . . ."

I waved my hands at the walls to indicate the ample space in her apartment.

"Just for tonight, that is," I added.

She cocked an eyebrow at me and said nothing.

"You have no idea what they did to my place. It looks like the morning after Godzilla's bachelor party."

She seemed to relent a bit, her eyes twinkling with amusement.

"Don't you have any friends who can put you up?"

"Oh, sure," I replied. "Lots. But none of them is what I'm looking for."

"Oh? And what are you looking for?"

"An admirer of Flaubert," I said. "Someone who feels great empathy with Madame Bovary."

She grinned and shook her head.

"What a dumb piece of dialogue that was."

"Yeah," I said, trying not to wince. "I wonder who made it up?"

"Not Jerry De Marco, that's for sure. He never even . . ."

"You know Jerry De Marco?"

"Yes. He's the guy I told you about, the one who got me into this."

"He's the one you used to go out with?"

"Just a few times. How do you know Jerry?"

"We go back a long way," I said stiffly. "He and I and Gloria."

She gazed at me coolly.

"I guess Gloria's his wife, is that it?"

"Yes."

"I see," she said frostily. She got up and walked into the kitchen. I followed her and stood in the doorway while she poured a second cup of coffee.

"Do you want to talk about it?" I asked.

"About what?" She kept her back to me.

"About you and Jerry."

"What is there to talk about? We met at a party and we were attracted to each other, that's all."

"You really go for silk shirts open to the navel? Lots of gold chains and hairy chest?"

"Oh, for Christ's sake." She brushed past me into the living room.

"Do you make a practice of going out with married men?" I called after her.

She turned brusquely to face me.

"It's none of your business what I make a practice of," she said angrily. "And I don't see what it has to do with the present situation."

"No, no," I replied hastily. "I shouldn't have said that."

"I think it was a mistake, your coming up here."

"No, don't say that. I really got out of line. I'm sorry."

Her face relaxed a bit.

"I guess I'm a little nervous," I explained. "Over everything that's been happening. So when you mentioned Jerry . . . well, he's the one who got me into this, too."

"Oh," she said softly. "Why would he do all that? What's behind it?"

"I don't know, but I'm beginning to think he's not a very nice person. I just don't like the thought of

someone like you being taken advantage of by someone like that."

"I already told you I stopped going out with him
when I found out he was married."

"Did you, er . . ."

I wanted to know if she had slept with him but
could hardly ask her that. She stared coolly at me,
waiting for me to finish my question. She seemed to
guess what was on my mind.

"Did you go out with him many times?"

She shrugged. "Four or five."

It had all happened before I knew her, I told myself. It didn't matter.

"I just wouldn't have thought he was your type," I
said lamely.

A glint of amusement flickered in her eyes.

"Let's just say I'm a pushover for the dark, Mediterranean type."

We Feinsteins, as it happens, are swarthy of skin
and dark of eye, so I assumed I was forgiven.

"Anyway, it's all in the past," I said. "I'm not going
to dwell on it."

"That's big of you," she replied.

"What about the other guy?" A strategic retreat to
the business at hand. "The one who said he was an
undercover cop."

"What about him?"

"Well, to start with, what did he look like?"

She frowned in concentration. It made her even
more beautiful.

"It's hard to say. He was kind of nondescript. Mid-
forties, I would say, not too tall, kind of wiry. The
type who just blends in with the crowd, you know?"

It did not sound like anyone I knew, or maybe it sounded like a lot of people I knew.

"He's so ordinary," she went on, "I almost didn't spot him up on Riverside Drive yesterday."

I sat bolt upright.

"He was on Riverside Drive yesterday?"

"Sure."

"You mean when we met? To arrange things?"

"Yes. Didn't I mention that? He was sitting two benches away from you when I got there."

"You mean you knew he was going to be there? You were looking for him?"

"Sure. I had no intention of going to meet a professional killer without someone on hand in case I needed help."

"He was there to protect you?"

"Partly. Mostly he was there to record our conversation."

"What?"

"To record our conversation. I told you, he said he was an undercover policeman trying to get evidence against a murder ring."

"Wait a minute. You mean the guy that hired you, the one Jerry introduced you to, is the same guy who taped our conversation in Riverside Park?"

"That's right. At the hotel, too. He had me report to him just before I went to your room. It did seem strange, him knowing about the hotel; before you even mentioned it, I mean. He seemed to know you were going to set a meeting at the Hotel Clayton."

"He knew that in advance?"

"Oh, yes. He told me that morning he would be in room 309. At the time I figured maybe that particular hotel was a regular meeting place. You know, for making contracts and things like that."

"What was his name?"

She frowned and shook her head.

"I can't remember."

"Did he look like Elisha Cook, Jr.?"

"Who's Elisha Cook, Jr.?"

"Did he have a stutter?"

"Yes! You know who he is!"

I nodded. "His name is Albert Lemay. He's a private investigator, some kind of surveillance expert. I think he's probably a shady character; at least he said his license had once been suspended. He seems to get most of his business from the mob."

She looked at me curiously. "Elliot, how do you know so much about these gangsters?"

I told her about my adventures of the night before.

"Oh my God!" she exclaimed when I had finished. "What a frightening experience. It must have been awful."

"Well, it was a little unnerving at times."

"A little unnerving? That's all?"

"My training as an actor helped me control my reactions."

She raised a quizzical eyebrow.

"I was scared out of my mind," I said.

"I don't wonder."

"Then on top of that to be threatened with a jail sentence and then find my apartment torn to pieces . . ."

"Jail sentence?" She looked alarmed. "What are you talking about?"

I told her about my interview with Appian Productions.

"Do you think they can really put us in jail?" she wanted to know.

"I wondered about that myself," I said. "I think it was mostly bluff, but you never know. There must be laws against giving and taking murder contracts, don't you think? Even if it's not for real."

She gazed at me thoughtfully for a few moments.

"Elliot, I'm scared. What do you suppose is behind it all?"

"I don't know. I've been trying to think about it, but I'm just too tired and tense. It's been a hell of a twenty-four hours."

"I'll bet it has." She nodded sympathetically. "No wonder you're tense. Come here, let me massage the back of your neck. I'm really good at that. I'm sure it will make you feel better."

I moved next to her on the couch and leaned back while she gently kneaded my shoulder muscles.

"Elliot, we have to stick together in this. Help each other."

"Through thick and thin," I assured her.

Her hands moved gently up my neck.

"I'm glad you're with me," she said. "It's very comforting."

I turned and reached up to her.

"That's friendship," I said, drawing her to me.

"The perfect blendship," she answered as our mouths met.

Some time in the middle of the night I woke and looked over at her. Her golden hair lay sprawled across the pillow; her face had the sweet, serious look of a little child. I leaned down and kissed her lightly. She purred and rubbed against me.

"Binky Bannerman," I thought, "eat your heart out."

13

I spent about an hour in Amanda's place before heading back to Mercer Street, drinking coffee and acclimating myself to my new surroundings. I strolled around the apartment trying to determine if my things would fit and whether our decorating tastes could coexist peacefully.

A life-size Fred and Ginger danced the Continental on the living-room wall, and that suited me fine. From opposite sides of the bathroom Dorothy and the Tin Man smiled at each other out of framed eight-by-ten glossies. It made me wince a bit, but I was prepared to make some concessions; it was, after all, only the bathroom. The bedroom, on the other hand, would have to be redone. The huge display—practically billboard size it was—of Julie Andrews cavorting through the Austrian Alps would have to come down. Just the right spot, I decided, for my Don Giovanni poster with the fetching picture of Kiri Te Kanawa. Or perhaps the one from the Rousseau exhibit at the Modern.

I figured we could work it out. At least she didn't hang pictures of herself on the wall.

It would have been enjoyable to stay there all day, loafing and reading and waiting for Amanda, but a start had to be made on the rebuilding of Phil Bender's apartment, a job which, if not in the class of post-

war Berlin, would nevertheless take time and money.
And, of course, I had a lot bigger supply of one of
those commodities than the other.

There was also the problem of the police. Amanda
was adamant in refusing to let me call them. No
harm had come to anyone, she insisted, and no pur-
pose would be served by subjecting her to police in-
terrogation, not to mention possible criminal charges.
If they were on to me, that was no reason for both of
us to take a rap (her phrase, not mine).

Well, of course I understood her desire for anonym-
ity, and it was hard to go against her wishes. Nobody
wants to play the stoolie and finger a buddy to the
coppers. On the other hand, Baily could be counted
on to take a dim view of my withholding such important information. And how did we really know that
no one had come to harm? There was Roxanne, for
instance. What had happened to her? The hiring of
Amanda to impersonate her seemed like an attempt
to cover up her disappearance and—who knew?—
maybe even her murder.

I thought about that during the subway ride downtown. Roxanne was suspected of stealing money from
the Tarabola organization. Lemay, who did a lot of
work for the mob, was employed to watch her. Perhaps he found out where she hid the loot, then killed
her for it. And what about Jerry? What was his part
in it? He was Roxanne's friend, God help her; her ex-
lover, if Bonello was right; maybe even her accomplice. It would not have been beyond him to betray
her to Lemay in return for a share of the money.
That might explain their employing Amanda—to
keep up the pretense that Roxanne was alive lest the
mob's suspicions turn in their direction.

But why stage a fake murder contract? And where did Barany fit in? It was too deep for me to fathom. I only knew that my best interests lay in keeping on Baily's good side and out of the way of the Tarabola mob.

It was with such thoughts that I approached the door of Phil Bender's apartment to find a visitor ringing the bell. A big, ugly character he was, dumb and mean looking; perfect casting for the title role in *Muzio: The Movie.* Had he worn a sign reading GANG-STER his business would not have been plainer.

"Hey!" he called out when he spotted me. "Ain't you Fenway?"

"I, er, yes, er, no, that is . . ."

He had caught me off guard. It isn't every day I find a gorilla in a tight-fitting polyester suit standing at my apartment door.

"Yes, I'm Fenway," I finally answered. "What about it?"

I was a little surprised to hear the belligerent note that had crept into my voice. I guess I was tired of being pushed around.

He lumbered the few yards down the hall to where I stood, then spent a moment looking me over.

"Is that your real name?" he finally asked.

"Oh, for Christ's sake, I'm tired of that question," I snapped. "You want to know my real name? It's Belker, Mick Belker. Fenway is just one of my many disguises."

My outburst seemed to amuse him. His thick upper lip curled into a moronic smile.

"Detective Belker to you, Dog-breath," I added.

"You through?" he asked equably.

"Yes, I'm through," I answered.

"You Fenway?"

"Yes, I'm Fenway."

He reached toward his hip pocket.

"What the hell do you guys want from me?" I asked. "Why don't you just leave me alone?"

He held open his wallet to display a police badge.

"Inspector Baily wants to see you at headquarters," he said.

"Where the hell have you been?" Baily asked sourly. "I've been trying to get hold of you all morning."

"I didn't realize I was under house arrest."

"Sit down," he commanded curtly. He turned to the Muzio clone who had brought me in. "Tell Agent Bonello the killer elite is here."

He took a package of Alka-Seltzer from his desk and dropped two tablets in a glass of water.

"Those things have a lot of sodium," I pointed out.

"You also impersonate doctors?" he asked.

Bonello was wearing an elegant pair of lightweight navy-blue trousers and a beautifully tailored grey linen jacket. He nodded coolly at me, walked behind the desk, and leaned against the wall in back of Baily.

"A man was murdered last night," said Baily, fixing a hard stare on me.

He paused as if expecting me to say something.

"Someone I know?" I asked inanely.

"A private detective named Albert Lemay. You remember him?"

"What?" The two men eyed me silently. "Lemay? Murdered? How awful."

"Then you do remember him," Baily said.

"Of course I remember him. He's the one they hired to follow Amanda. I mean Roxanne."

"Who's Amanda?" asked Bonello, instantly alert.

"Why was he killed?" I tried to ignore the last question.

"We thought maybe you could help us answer that one," said Baily.

"Me? How should I know?"

"Who's Amanda?" Bonello persisted.

"She's, er . . . It's, er, it's a long story," I stammered.

"We've got time."

I glanced uncomfortably from one man to the other. Neither looked very sympathetic.

"Let me fill you in on Lemay." Baily's voice was gruff, cold, matter-of-fact. "His body was found early this morning in a car parked off the Belt Parkway near the Verrazano Bridge. Shot two times in the head. The medical examiner places the time of death between midnight and four A.M. Where were you last night, by the way?"

"This is crazy," I protested. "I had nothing to do with Lemay's death. I didn't even know him. Why should I kill him?"

"Just answer the question. Where were you last night?"

"I spent the night with a friend."

"All night?"

"Yes. All night."

"And will he or she be willing to testify to that?"

"She," I said. "And yes, I suppose so, if it's necessary."

"She," he repeated approvingly. "Well, good for you, Elliot. You're not as degenerate as I thought."

"What do you want with me?" I asked. "You can't seriously believe I had anything to do with Lemay's death."

Baily stared coldly at me.

"The murder weapon was found a few hours ago," he said. "In a clump of weeds near the entrance to the parkway." He paused for dramatic effect. "It was a .22 caliber pistol."

I had an uncomfortable feeling I knew what was coming next.

"Upon checking the pistol we found that it's registered to a Philip J. Bender of 180 Mercer Street. Quite a coincidence, don't you think?"

My mouth was very dry. "Could I have a glass of water?"

"Sure. You want a couple of Alka-Seltzer? Oh no, I forgot; they have too much sodium."

"Phil Bender is the guy I sublet from," I explained after taking a few sips. "He doesn't have anything to do with this. He's out on the West Coast."

"We already checked that out," said Baily.

"My apartment was ransacked yesterday, torn apart from top to bottom. Whoever did it took the gun."

The two men exchanged glances.

"Your apartment was ransacked?" Baily asked. "What time was that?"

"I don't know exactly. I found it that way when I got home around four."

"Did you report it to the police?"

"Well, no, not right away."

"Not right away? You mean you did it later?"

"I mean I was going to do it, but something else came up and I didn't get the chance."

"What came up?"

"I, er, got a call from a friend and went to visit her."

"Oh, come on, Elliot. You say your place was torn apart from top to bottom—those were your words, weren't they? And then you right away got so distracted by a call from some lady friend you forgot all about it until just now?"

"The call was important."

"Oh? What was it about?"

"It was personal."

There was a long silence during which they both stared sternly at me. It was broken by Bonello.

"I'm sorry you won't help us. I had hoped that by being open with you, taking you into our confidence, we could count on your cooperation. It seems to have been a mistake." He turned to Baily. "You were right, Walt. It would have been better to book him yesterday and let him sweat it out in jail for a while."

"Book me for what? I didn't do anything."

"There's fraud and larceny," said Baily harshly, "as well as consorting with known criminals. I think we can get you at least two years."

"Why are you doing this to me? What do you want?"

"Just the truth," said Bonello quietly. He stared coolly at me. "Who's Amanda."

I looked from one to the other. If *mercy falleth like the gentle rain from heaven* they were equipped with wide umbrellas.

"Amanda is an actress," I said. "She's the one who impersonated Roxanne, the one who hired me to kill John Barany."

"An actress?" Baily exploded. "What the hell is

this, a criminal investigation or a miniseries?" He glared at me. "What's her angle?"

"She doesn't have any angle," I insisted. "She's a victim in this, just like me."

"A victim?" He snorted. "You have a funny idea about what constitutes a victim. A second-story man whose ladder breaks, for instance, is not a victim."

"She was being used, the same as I was."

"Used?" Bonello asked sharply. "Who was using her?"

"Lemay and Jerry De Marco," I replied. "They hired her to impersonate Roxanne. They told her Lemay was an undercover cop investigating a murder ring."

"Lemay and De Marco?" He sounded surprised. "Working together? Are you sure about that?"

"Yes."

"How do you know it was them?" Bonello asked.

"She told me. She knows Jerry, and there was no mistaking her description of Lemay."

The two men fell into thoughtful silence.

"If Roxanne was skimming money, as Nero thinks," said Bonello after a bit, "then it's a good bet Jerry was in it with her."

"That's right," the other agreed. "And now it seems he was working both sides of the street, selling her out to the Tarabola mob."

Bonello shook his head. "I don't think so. If that's what he was doing he wouldn't have engaged an actress to impersonate her. It's more likely he and Lemay were working some scam of their own."

"Yes, of course," Baily agreed. "He must have helped Lemay find out where she was keeping the money . . ."

"And the notebook," Bonello put in.

"And the notebook," repeated Baily.

"Notebook?" I asked. "What notebook?"

"Then they got rid of Roxanne," Baily continued, ignoring me. "And hired an actress as a cover-up."

"That's just what I was thinking!" I cried excitedly.

Baily grimaced. "How encouraging," he said acidly.

"Jerry knew I kept a gun in the apartment," I went on. "He probably broke in and stole it and killed Lemay with it."

"Why would he want to kill Lemay?" Bonello asked.

"So he wouldn't have to share the money, I guess. Or maybe they had a falling-out."

Bonello shook his head.

"I don't think so. You said your place was torn apart, didn't you?"

"Yes. Upholstery slashed, bookcases emptied; the whole place was turned upside down."

"That's not the way you go about looking for a gun. A gun isn't likely to be concealed in upholstery cushions. They were looking for something else."

"They?"

"Your friends from Tozzi's."

"But what would they have been looking for in my apartment?"

"Roxanne is said to have kept a notebook," Bonello explained. "A ledger of all the transactions she was involved in, complete with names and dates. If that's true, there could be enough information in it to put Frank Tarabola and some of the others away for tax evasion."

"But why would they think I had it?"

"They aren't sure exactly what your role is in this business. They're not entirely convinced you're just an innocent actor roped into a con game. For all they know you could be an accomplice."

"That's ridiculous," I protested.

"They don't want to take any chances. They must have gone through your place looking for the notebook, taken the gun, and used it on Lemay."

"Which means," added Baily, "that they must have found out Lemay was double-crossing them. I wouldn't be surprised if your friend Jerry De Marco turns up dead, too."

I was struck by a chilling thought.

"What about Amanda?" I asked. "You don't think they'll do anything to her, do you?"

"It's possible," Baily answered. "I think we'd better put her under protective custody. Where is she now?"

"I don't know," I said uncomfortably. "She went out for the day."

"Out where?"

"I don't know exactly. She said she'd be back around five."

Baily glowered at me. "You were supposed to call us as soon as you heard from her."

"I, uh . . ."

I was saved from his ire by the ringing of the telephone.

"Baily," he growled into the mouthpiece. Whatever he heard jolted him into a stiff, upright position in his chair. "When?" he barked. Then, after a pause, "Any witnesses?" Another pause. "Did you get a description?" He swung around and glared at me. "All right, we're on our way."

He hung up the phone, jumped out of his chair, and walked quickly to the door, stopping to grab a rumpled seersucker jacket from the coat rack nearby.

"Come on," he called over his shoulder.

"What's up?" Bonello asked.

"Frank Tarabola was shot to death half an hour ago right outside the Baron's apartment house. Barany himself took a bullet in the shoulder. He's at St. Luke's in fair condition."

He was out the door before he finished speaking, with Bonello right behind him. I hurried out of the room and shouted down the hallway after them.

"Hey! What about me?"

"You come too." Baily called back without turning around.

I caught up to them at the elevator.

"Tarabola and Eraldo Giusti had lunch at Barany's place," Baily explained when I arrived. "The three of them left the building together. As soon as they stepped outside, some broad got out of a car and fired a couple of shots at them." He turned to face me. "Where did you say that actress went?"

"I don't know exactly. A dance class, I think, and a photo session. Why?"

"Because the witnesses, as usual, give contradictory accounts of what they saw, but they all agree in their descriptions of the killer."

He paused and looked at me.

"A tall, good-looking woman with long, blonde hair."

They kept me with them through the rest of the afternoon; first at the scene of the crime, then later at the hospital. Mostly I sat in the car while they interviewed witnesses and supervised a squad of technicians taking measurements and photographs. Once, sitting in a waiting room at St. Luke's, I caught a glimpse of a pale, fragile-looking Don Eraldo being conducted down a corridor by a couple of uniformed policemen.

Tarabola had been shot in the chest and died before the ambulance arrived. Barany was out of danger. The bullet that had penetrated his right shoulder had missed the bone, and he was expected to be up and about in a matter of days. Don Eraldo, after being treated for shock, was released at his own insistence against the advice of the physician on duty.

From snatches of conversation I pieced together a few of the facts. The assailant's car had been a dark blue, late-model Buick Regal, according to the doorman, who was able to give the police part of the license number. The woman herself was tall, slender, and long limbed. About her age the witnesses disagreed, placing it anywhere between mid-twenties and mid-forties. But they were unanimous on one point: she had striking hair, long and golden.

"It could have been a wig," I pointed out to Baily on the way to the hospital.

"Thanks for the tip," he said dryly.

"Besides, there must be a million women in New York with long, blonde hair."

"Look," he said curtly, "I brought you along to keep an eye on you. Not as a consultant."

The Buick had been standing in front of the entrance, double-parked with the engine running, when the three men came out of the building. The killer had emerged as soon as the first one, Don Eraldo, appeared, then waited while Barany held the door for Tarabola to precede him. Not until Barany had stepped out did she fire. The first shot dropped Tarabola; the second hit the Baron. Two of the witnesses stated that both shots seemed aimed at Barany, and that Tarabola had been hit by mistake.

That was all the information they got as far as I could tell, but it took all afternoon to get it. At the end of the day, around five o'clock, they took me home. Both of them came upstairs to survey the apartment, bringing along two of Baily's assistants to take pictures and dust for prints.

"Not that there'll be any," said Baily sourly.

Finally they left me alone after taking Amanda's address and phone number and instructing me to contact them as soon as I heard from her.

For about an hour and a half after they left I tried to straighten out the apartment, stopping every fifteen minutes or so to call Amanda. It began to drive me crazy. One time I let the phone ring thirty times.

Just when I had made up my mind to go uptown and wait in front of her building she called me.

"Where the hell are you?" I asked frantically.

"Just a few blocks away, as a matter of fact. In a

restaurant on Mulberry Street. Could you come over?"

"A restaurant on Mulberry Street?"

"Yes. It's called Paolo's."

"What are you doing there?"

"I'll explain when I see you. Can you come?"

"Yes, of course. I'll be right over. Are you all right?"

"Yes, I'm fine. Did you speak to those policemen?"

"Are you kidding? I've been with them all afternoon."

"Did you tell them about me? Who I really am and all?"

"Yes. I had to. Listen, Amanda, things have gotten pretty grim. A couple of people have been shot."

"I know. That's why I'm here."

"What do you mean?"

"You'll see when you get here."

"Uh, listen, I'm supposed to call the police as soon as I hear from you."

"Oh. Well, don't do that, okay? It will only make things worse."

"Make things worse? What do you mean?"

"Elliot, please. Don't ask questions. Just come over here and don't call the police. It will only cause trouble."

"Uh, Amanda, you didn't, er . . . I mean it wasn't you . . ."

"Are you crazy? Of course not. How could you even think such a thing?"

"It's just that the killer was a tall woman with long blonde hair."

"Well, it wasn't me. Do I seem like a killer to you?"

Indeed she did not. I mean she was awfully pretty.

And in bed the night before she had looked so innocent, so vulnerable. On the other hand, what did I
know? I had never slept with a murderer. Maybe they
all looked that way.

"Elliot, please."

"Okay," I said.

"Ask the maitre d' for the Nero party."

"What?"

"I have to go." And with that she hung up.

My heart was pounding, my breath came quick and
short. I paced the living room, trying to resolve my
uncertainty. Prudence dictated I call Baily; indeed, it
seemed the only sensible thing to do. On the other
hand Amanda had been very insistent, and I had
more or less given her my word. For a few minutes I
hovered over the telephone, staring irresolutely at the
number Bonello had given me. Then I stuffed his
card back in my wallet, left the apartment, and
walked quickly toward Mulberry Street.

A dumb thing to do, no doubt. Tarabola was dead
and so was Lemay. Barany was in the hospital, shot
by a tall woman with long, blonde hair. The police
had instructed me to let them know when I heard
from Amanda, and there she was a few blocks away
dining with gangsters. And I, poor fool, was hurry-
ing to meet her.

But, says Shakespeare: *Virtue is bold and goodness
never fearful.* And I have always been a sucker for
blondes with green eyes.

The Nero party was breaking bread in a courtyard
in back of the restaurant, a little walled-in patio lit by
a string of Japanese lanterns and two flaming torches
that gave off a smell of insect repellent. The patio

held two tables, a small one near the entrance and a larger round one in the center. Vinnie and Muzio sat stiffly at the former, watching me warily as I stepped through the doorway from the restaurant. Vinnie's look was cold and unfriendly, but Muzio curled his lip in a slight smile of salute to the man who had seduced Lisa Duncan.

At either end of the far wall Don Eraldo's bodyguards stood like bridge pylons. Amanda sat at the main table, flanked by Nero and the Don and, next to them, Louie the Horse and Willie the Rabbit. Nero motioned to an empty seat opposite him.

"Please sit down," he said, the soul of courtesy.

I remained standing. "You guys think that because you have a lot of muscle you can push everyone around. I'm tired of being carted off to Italian restaurants every time you feel like a chat."

"Carted?" A glint of amusement flickered briefly in Nero's eyes. "I thought you walked here."

"There are laws against abducting people."

"No one has been abducted."

"What about . . ."

"Miss Cole agreed to have dinner with us and help with an investigation we're conducting." He smiled condescendingly. "That hardly qualifies as abduction."

I looked at Amanda, who nodded briefly in confirmation. She looked a bit wan and disheveled, but not in great distress. The slight touch of disarray made her even more beautiful, and I noticed that Don Eraldo thought so too, for he never took his eyes off her.

"Now please sit down," Nero went on smoothly. "Have something to eat. I recommend the veal pizzaiola."

The place was certainly an improvement over Toz-zi's. No fish heads, for one thing. No Frank Tarabola, for another. I sat down but declined to eat.

"Miss Cole has told us that both of you were brought into this business by Jerry De Marco. Would you confirm that, please?"

I glanced at Amanda. She shrugged.

"Believe me," said Nero, "it's not in your interest to protect De Marco. He's not looking out for you."

I remained silent, unsure of what to do.

"This isn't a game, Fenway." His tone became sharper. "My father-in-law has been killed."

"That's a matter for the police," I replied.

Once again a small spark of amusement flashed briefly in his eyes.

"Their interests and ours don't altogether coincide," he said. "And I don't have much confidence in either their methods or their sense of retribution."

"Michael, you're wasting your time." Louie Cavallo sounded as if his larynx needed a valve job. "Let Muzio take the bastard for a ride and explain things to him. Maybe that will make him more agreeable."

Nero stared at me, his eyebrows raised. "Well?"

He was right. I owed nothing to Jerry De Marco.

"Okay, yes, it was Jerry who set me up."

"Tell me about it."

I recounted my meeting with Jerry. When I was done Nero took a thin plastic portfolio from under his seat and extracted several photographs.

"What about her?" He pushed over an eight-by-ten of Roxanne. "Have you ever seen her?"

"The police showed me her picture yesterday. That's the only time I ever saw her."

"How about this one?" It was a picture of Mrs. Barany.

"Same thing," I replied. "All I ever saw was her picture."

"Think hard. You're sure you never saw her with De Marco?"

"I'm positive."

Nero sat back and looked round at the others. "Anybody have any questions?"

The Don coughed lightly. There was a respectful silence.

"Do you like opera?" he asked, speaking directly to Amanda.

"Huh? Oh, no."

"Ah." He nodded sadly.

"That is, I don't really know anything about it," she added hastily.

"Ah." He smiled.

"I like musical comedy," she said accommodatingly.

"They think that Jerry's behind it," she told me later, when we were by ourselves.

"So do the police," I said. "It seems like a pretty safe bet."

"I overheard them talking when I came back from the phone. They think some woman named Marie did the actual shooting."

"That would be Mrs. Barany," I said. "She and Jerry were lovers. They must have wanted to kill Barany and throw the blame on Roxanne. Shooting Tarabola was probably an accident."

We were in a delicatessen on Columbus Avenue,

and I had just ordered a double pastrami sandwich with cream soda and a side of potato salad.

"God, I'm hungry," I growled. "I wish they'd hurry."

"Why on earth didn't you eat when we were at Paolo's?"

"Are you kidding? With Louie Cavallo? He's the biggest appetite suppressant since Dexatrim."

"Michael says that Paolo's has the best Italian food in the city."

"Michael? You mean Nero?"

"He told me to call him Michael."

"Oh, great. Next he'll probably ask you to be his moll."

"What's a moll?"

"You don't know what a moll is? Don't you ever watch James Cagney movies? His girlfriend."

"Don't be ridiculous. He's not my type. Besides, he's all wrapped up in his family. He showed me pictures of his two little boys. They're adorable."

"I'll bet. They probably each have their own little junior garrotes."

"What are garrotes?"

"Never mind," I said.

"Did you think it was wrong?" she asked. "Telling them about Jerry, I mean."

I shook my head. "They would have found out anyway."

"I don't think we owe him anything." She sounded as if she were trying to convince herself.

My sandwich came and I dove into it.

"Elliot." She picked halfheartedly at a piece of apple strudel.

"What?"

"What do you think they'll do to him?"

"Not while I'm eating, okay?"

A worried little frown darkened her gorgeous features.

"I'm sure he'll make a fine cornerstone," I said.

Which sounded pretty glib, but when I thought about it I felt awful. Jerry had turned out to be a first-class rat, but we had known each other in happier times.

Where be your gibes now?, I thought. *Your gambols? Your songs? Your men with five penises that were wont to set the tables on a roar?*

Not a knockout as eulogies went, but I was not at my best. It had been a hell of a day.

We walked to her apartment hand in hand. At the corner of seventy-fourth and Amsterdam, waiting for a traffic light, she leaned against me and I kissed her.

"I love you," I whispered. She shook her head. "Don't make it serious," she said.

Her apartment was in total darkness.

"Why did you pull the shades down?" she asked.

"I didn't."

"You must have. Otherwise there'd be more light from the street." She switched on a lamp. "See?"

She walked to the window.

"Leave the shades alone!" A husky voice, taut with fear, came from the direction of the bedroom. We both turned toward it.

Jerry stood in the doorway, holding a gun.

15

He moved out of the doorway and along the living-room wall, away from the windows, keeping his eyes and the gun fixed on us as he went. He stopped when he reached a large upholstered chair and perched against one of its arms.

"Sit down," he said gruffly, motioning with the gun to the couch opposite him.

He looked haggard and unkempt, his eyes red, his body stiff with tension. Over his shoulder Fred and Ginger smiled at us, carefree and elegant in their frozen dance-step on the living room wall.

"Is anybody with you? Are you expecting anyone?" His voice had an edge of hysteria.

"Jerry . . ." My mouth was very dry.

"Just answer my question."

"No, nobody."

"Did you notice anybody hanging around outside?"

"No. Listen, Jerry, you're making a big mistake. Why don't you put away the gun . . ."

"Shut up, Elliot. I don't need any stupid advice."

"We're your friends. We want to help you."

"Shut up!" His voice was charged with a quick surge of energy which ebbed immediately. "I need some help," he said weakly.

"That's what I'm saying. Just put away the gun."

"No!" He jabbed it forward, pointing at my mid-section. I saw that his hand was trembling. "Don't push me, Elliot. Please."

Tears formed in his eyes. He rubbed them away roughly with his free hand.

"What do you want with us?" Amanda's voice was surprisingly calm. The look she fixed on Jerry was cool and level, her agitation betrayed only by a tightness at the corners of her eyes and a slight trembling of the hands she held folded in her lap.

"What time is it?" Jerry asked.

I looked at my watch. "A few minutes after ten."

"I need a drink," he said to Amanda. "Do you have any Bourbon?"

She shook her head. "There's some Canadian Club," she said. "And a little Scotch."

"Where do you keep it?"

"In the kitchen."

He stood up. "Get me some Scotch. But walk slow, so I can keep you in sight. Elliot, you stay on the couch."

He followed her, moving sideways, positioning himself so that he could watch her through the kitchen doorway while keeping an eye on the couch. He stood there jiggling his leg nervously until she came out with a half-full tumbler.

"That's all there is," she said. He downed most of the liquid in one long gulp.

"You gotta help get me out of here," he said.

"What do you want us to do?" I asked.

He drained the tumbler without replying, then moved sideways to the window, watching us as he went.

"Sit down," he said, motioning to the couch.

He stood against the wall next to the window try-ing to look past the edge of the shade and catch a glimpse of the street below. For an instant, as he stepped closer to the window and lifted the shade ever so slightly to get a better view, his attention left us, and I might have rushed him had I been more daring. But I hesitated and the moment passed.

"I said sit down." He turned back to us and made a jerking motion toward the couch with his gun hand. We did as he ordered. He backed over to the armchair and dropped down wearily. "We'll wait a while and make sure everything is quiet outside."

"What do you want from us?" asked Amanda.

"There's a car," he said. "It's in a parking lot near the Lincoln Tunnel. I want Elliot to get it and bring it here."

As he spoke he shifted the gun to his left hand and dug in his pants pocket with his right, removing a set of keys and a parking stub.

"Here." He leaned forward and tossed them onto the floor at my feet.

The stub was from a lot on West Thirty-nineth Street. The key ring had a tag identifying the owner as Marie Barany, with an address on Central Park West.

"Let me guess," I said. "The car is a Buick Regal; late model, dark blue."

"What are you talking about?" Jerry spoke in an irritated tone, his face in a pained frown as if he had a headache.

"That's the car Marie Barany was driving when she shot her husband and Frank Tarabola," I ex-plained to Amanda. "The doorman got part of the license number," I added to Jerry. "The police have probably checked it out by now."

He expelled his breath in a snorting sound that turned into a burst of dry, mirthless laughter.

"You've got it all figured out, huh?"

"I was with the police all afternoon," I said. "It seems to be the only explanation. You and she must have planned to kill Barany and put the blame on Roxanne. You used Lemay to get rid of her, then set me and Amanda up to make it look like she was still alive and out to get Barany. That way you could make it look like she shot Barany, and you could even keep the money she stole from the mob."

"Whatever you say, Elliot. Just get me the car." He sounded tired, defeated; the voice of a man hanging on by a thread. "It's a cream-colored Chrysler New Yorker. The license number is on the tag."

He rubbed his eyes wearily. His hands, I noticed, had begun to tremble again.

"Are you telling me that's not what happened?" I asked. "That Marie Barany didn't shoot her husband?"

"I don't want to talk about it."

"Why else would you have set up that scene between me and Amanda? It doesn't make sense unless . . ."

"I don't want to talk about it!" His voice trembled. He glared at me in silence for a few moments, then began blinking rapidly. Tears formed in his eyes. "That's the way it was supposed to happen, but things got screwed up. It all came off one day too soon."

"A day too soon? What do you mean?"

"We got double-crossed. Somebody jumped the gun on us."

"Double-crossed? By whom?"

"I don't know. Everybody. That little bastard Lemay."

"Lemay is dead, Jerry. He was shot last night."

He seemed at first not to hear what I said, staring vacantly at me, lost in thought. Then he nodded his head repeatedly, a series of short jerks that spread to a jiggling motion throughout his upper torso.

"Yeah, yeah, that figures. They're really out for blood." He rubbed his hands over his eyes. "Oh, Christ, I'm in trouble."

Amanda spoke in a soft, cool voice. "If you're really in trouble, why don't you let us help you?" She sounded calm and very reasonable, though I noticed how pale her face had become. Her hands had stopped trembling and were clenched tightly together in her lap, so tight that her knuckles were white. "Elliot knows these policemen . . ."

Her voice trailed off as a spasm of dry, grim laughter came from Jerry. In the middle of it he began to sniffle and rub his eyes. After a minute or so he stopped rubbing, took a long, deep breath, and seemed to gain control of himself.

"Enough talk," he said decisively. "I gotta get out of here. Elliot, go get the car."

He walked over to the window and peered around the edge of the shade.

"When you get back here, ride around the block a couple of times to make sure nobody's following you. Then park the car in front of the house. There's a hydrant there; I saw it when I came in. You can park right in that space. Then go to the pay phone on the corner of Amsterdam and call me here. Leave the keys in the car."

"What about Amanda?" I asked.

"She stays here with me until you call."

"And then what happens?"

"I go down to the car and drive away. You wait till I'm clear, then come back up here."

"That's all?"

"That's all. Nobody gets hurt."

I hesitated.

"Let Amanda come with me," I said.

"Are you crazy? You think I'm going to let the two of you walk out of here?"

"You'd better go, Elliot." Amanda's voice was firm, but she spoke slowly, as if with great effort to keep control. "The sooner you get back here, the sooner it'll be over."

"I don't like to leave you."

"I'll be all right. Jerry won't hurt me, will you, Jerry?"

"No. Not as long as Elliot gets the car." His voice choked. "Elliot, I'm under a big strain. Don't push me over the edge."

I looked at Amanda. She nodded solemnly. "Go," she said softly.

It was almost eleven when I got to the lot. The street was dark and still, the only touch of life being the little glow of light from the parking attendant's booth. There was no sign of anyone within.

I paid the taxi and watched it drive away, feeling my heart pump up into my throat. Along the wall next to the parking-lot fence stood a large cardboard carton. A dirty, ragged old man lay curled up inside,

eyes open, watching me as I walked around the rail-
road gate that barred the driveway into the lot.

"Hello!" I called. "Anybody in charge, here?"

No answer.

I walked up and down two rows of silent, spooky
cars before spotting the Chrysler. As I bent down to
check the license number I saw that the left rear tire
was flat.

I kicked the wheel and pounded my fist on the
trunk in frustration. The sound reverberated in the
eerie stillness, and I looked nervously around. There
was nothing in sight but rows of cars, inert and silent
in the dark.

I took a few deep breaths to calm myself, then
opened the trunk of the Chrysler. Inside, over the
well where the spare tire sat, was a small overnight
case. I started to lift it out of the way, then, on impulse, put it back down and opened it. The contents
took my breath away.

The case was filled with money.

Twenty-dollar bills, bound in packets. There must
have been a couple of hundred packets, maybe a quar-
ter of a million dollars, more money than I had ever
dreamed of. It was hard to believe it was just sitting
there in the trunk of a car in some dreary parking lot
on West 39th Street.

I grabbed a couple of packets and examined them
under the light of the trunk lid. Crisp, new twenty-
dollar bills; about fifty in each stack, it looked like. As
I put them back in the overnight case I noticed something sticking out of a pocket on the inner side of the
lid. I pulled it out and held it under the light.

It was a small notebook with blue cloth covers.

"Hey! You!" A voice from the row behind me, not

very loud but menacing. I threw the notebook into the trunk and slammed the lid quickly, then spun around to see who was there.

Facing me was a tall, barrel-chested man of about forty years. In his hand he had a tire iron.

"This your car?" he asked suspiciously.

"Yes!" I shouted. "That is, er, yes. Here are the keys, see?"

"You got the ticket for it?"

"Yes. Oh yes." I fumbled in my pocket for it. "Here it is."

He took a miniature flashlight out of his coverall pocket and aimed it at the keys in my left hand and the parking stub in my right.

"You got a flat tire," he said.

"Uh, yes, I know. I was just about to change it."

"I'll give you a hand. You got a jack in the trunk?"

"No. Er, that is, yes. I mean yes, I have a jack, but no, I don't need any help. Uh, thanks anyway."

He gazed at me with a flat, impassive look. "You don't want no help?"

"I don't get much exercise," I said.

He shrugged. "Suit yourself."

I drove up Tenth Avenue, trying to keep an eye open for any car that might be following me, but it was impossible to tell. In the movies or on TV the guys like Mike Hammer and Philip Marlowe sense that someone is following them by picking up his headlights in the rear-view mirror, but I've never been able to figure out how they do it. To me one set of headlights in the rear-view mirror looks pretty much like another. At any rate I managed to make it up to Amsterdam and 74th without being stopped or sideswiped or shot at, which, considering the way things had been going the last few days, was a better-than-average outing.

To tell the truth, I did stop once of my own accord. I could not resist another look at the treasure in the trunk. A quick glance was all I intended, just to make sure I had not imagined it, but before I zipped the overnight case shut I did pocket a fistful of dollars. After all, I had expenses to cover; restoring Phil's furniture alone would cost over a thousand. And with all that money who would miss one or two measly packets of twenties?

As an afterthought I also took the notebook. It might prove a useful bargaining tool if push came to shove. As I slipped it into my back pocket the thought occurred to me that Jerry might have had the same intention, and in terms of pushes and shoves he was probably a lot closer to the line of scrimmage than I was. But the way I saw it, it was every man for himself. As Raven said, you had to be careful.

I circled the block twice as instructed without seeing anything untoward, so I parked the car next to the hydrant and got out. The lights were on in Amanda's flat, but the shades were down, and I did not see any moving shadows. I walked to the corner and called Jerry.

"What the hell took you so long? I was going crazy."

"I had, uh . . . It's a long story. Is Amanda all right?"

"Yeah, she's fine. Did anybody follow you?"

"No, I don't think so."

"Did you park it next to the hydrant?"

"Yes."

"Did you leave the keys in it?"

"Yes."

"Then that's it. You hang around for about five minutes until I get clear of here, then you can come back."

"Okay. Uh, Jerry?"

"Yeah?"

"Good luck."

"Oh. Yeah, thanks. Well, what the hell—it's like the guy who jumped off the twenty-story building, you know? When he reached the nineteenth floor they heard him say 'So far, so good.' Take care of yourself, Elliot."

After he hung up I felt kind of numb. I stood with the dead receiver to my ear, staring vacantly at the little push buttons on the phone. It felt like some chapter of my life had just ended.

I was snapped out of my reverie by the feel of something hard prodding my back. At the same time a hand gripped my arm and a soft voice spoke in my ear.

"Don't turn around." The tone left no room for argument.

"Listen carefully." It was a no-nonsense voice, one used to being obeyed. A man's voice, but none I recognized. "When I tell you to go, you back up two steps, then turn and walk north on Amsterdam. Don't turn around, just walk straight ahead and keep your eyes in front of you."

"I, uh . . ."

"Keep walking for fifteen minutes, then you can go home."

"Uh, listen . . ."

"Where are the keys to the Chrysler?"

The object against my back pressed a little harder.

"I left them in the car."

"Okay. Go."

The grip on my arm was released and the pressure in my back was removed.

"Listen, there's a woman up there . . ."

"She'll be all right as long as no one tries anything stupid. We just want to borrow the car and have a talk with your friend Jerry. Now I'm not going to tell you again. Go."

I backed up two steps, expecting to collide with whoever was behind me, but he had moved out of the way. With my eyes focused rigidly in front of me I turned stiffly and walked slowly up Amsterdam Avenue. My legs were shaking and I found it hard to breathe. Halfway up the block I thought I was going to faint, and I leaned against a storefront for support.

As I straightened up I saw a cream-colored car that looked like a Chrysler drive slowly by. There looked to be four men in it, two in front, two in back. As it passed under a streetlamp I thought I saw one of the men in the rear seat, the one on my side, turn and look out the window. He looked like Jerry and he looked scared; but it was too far away to tell for sure.

16

"Who is Teresa?" Amanda asked me over Sunday breakfast.

"Huh?"

"Who is Teresa?"

She looked beautiful in the morning, her hair a soft gold, her face puffy with sleep like a child's.

"A girl I know," I answered. "My agent's secretary, actually. Why?"

"You woke up in the middle of the night, sat bolt upright in bed and shouted 'Oh my God! Teresa!' I just wondered who she was, that's all."

"Oh my God!" I exclaimed. "Teresa!"

"Yes," said Amanda. "Exactly like that."

"I was supposed to go out with her Friday night."

"Oh. Is she somebody special?"

"No, no," I said hastily. "Just a girl. My agent's secretary."

"They can be very helpful."

"I suppose. I don't want to talk about her right now. I want to talk about us." I gazed lovingly at her. "About last night. About tomorrow. About forever."

"That's certainly a lot to talk about."

"I love you," I declared fervently.

"You're sweet, but it's a little too early to talk about love, don't you think? Would you pass me the jam?"

I handed it to her.

"Right now I can't think about anything," she said as she spread jam on an English muffin, "except how good it feels to have that horrid business over with."

"It's certainly a relief," I agreed. "I hope we've heard the last of it."

"Tony says the police won't bother us."

"Tony?"

"You know, Agent Bonello. He says they're not going to press any charges against us."

"Since when did he become Tony?"

"That's what he told me to call him."

"He really came on strong, didn't he? I heard him offer to show you around Washington if you ever came down."

"He was just being friendly."

"He wasn't so goddamned friendly to me."

"Why, Elliot, you're jealous!" She grinned her dazzling white grin. "I think that's sweet."

I took a vicious bite out of my bagel.

"Come on, Elliot. He's not really my type."

"Oh no? Well, you sure gave a convincing performance yesterday."

The previous day had been spent in interviews with the police. We had both signed written statements and were told to stay available as witnesses, although it was doubtful we would ever be called to testify. Jerry and Marie Barany were both missing; almost certainly in the hands of Tarabola's lieutenants, according to Baily, who did not have much hope of finding them alive.

The case against those two seemed airtight. The police had found a half-burnt blonde wig in the incinerator of Barany's apartment building. The Buick Regal turned out to be a rental, charged on a credit card in Jerry De Marco's name. The car itself was found parked under the West Side Highway late Saturday afternoon, with the murder weapon locked in the glove compartment. The gun was registered to Marie Barany.

"Poor Jerry," Amanda said with a sigh. "In spite of everything, I can't help feeling sorry for him."

"Yes," I agreed. "I know what you mean."

"Elliot." She looked at me with a puzzled frown. "What do you suppose he meant when he said they were double-crossed?"

"I don't know," I said. "I wondered about that myself."

"He said somebody jumped the gun or something like that. What do you suppose that was all about?"

"I don't know. Did you mention it to the police?"

"Yes, I told Inspector Baily about it." I noticed that Baily was about the only male connected with the affair with whom she had not gotten on a first-name basis. "He said it wasn't important, that Jerry was probably lying."

Somehow I didn't think so, but it wasn't worth pursuing.

"Well," I said, "if he's satisfied why shouldn't we be? Come on, let's get our minds off it. I'll tell you what. Let me give you the Fenway WOMD Test."

"The Fenway what test? What are you talking about?"

"WOMD. Woman of my Dreams. To see if you qualify."

"Oh, Elliot, really!"

"Just answer yes or no to the following questions. One: Could you be happy in Cranston, Rhode Island as the wife of the heir to a plumbing supply business?"

"No, of course not."

"Good! Two: Could you be happy living in New York with an actor who doesn't know where his next job is coming from but is full of *joie de vivre?*"

"I guess it would depend on who the actor is."

"Fair enough. How about one of those dark, Mediterranean types?"

She smiled in spite of herself. "That would help," she said.

"Now you're getting in the spirit. Three—this is important: Do you like to eat Chinese food in bed?"

"You already asked me that once. I don't even like Chinese food."

"That's going too far, but we can work it out. Four: What do you think of Barry Manilow?"

"Yuck."

"Fantastic! You got a perfect score. You're the woman of my dreams."

"I'm honored."

"Let's live together. Think how happy we could be in this wonderful apartment."

"Only till September," she said.

"What?"

"It's a sublet. I have to be out by the end of the summer."

"Oh." That was a blow, but I rallied nicely. "It doesn't matter. Let's live here till the end of the summer. We can find a place by then."

"Don't you have an apartment?" she asked.

"Only till Friday."

She ate the rest of the English muffin without speaking.

"I realize what a great honor it is to have passed your test," she said after a while. There was a definite note of sarcasm in her voice. "To think that I was chosen out of all the women in New York . . ."

"Amanda, I love you," I said as simply as I could. "I think we could be great together."

"I like you a lot, Elliot," she replied. "But don't rush me, okay?"

The Chrysler was found a week later in a parking lot in Greenpoint, with Jerry's body in the trunk. I spent the next few days helping Gloria make arrangements for the funeral, a small service attended by a handful of Jerry's show-biz buddies. None of the underworld came to pay its respects. Afterward we went back to her apartment.

"Thanks, Elliot," she said. "I don't know what I would have done without you."

"Are you all right?"

"Yes, I think so. It was a big shock, of course. But there's no use pretending there was anything between us. That ended years ago."

"What will you do now?"

"Go back to Montana, I guess."

She made coffee and we took it to the living room.

"I'm surprised John Barany didn't come to the funeral," I said when we were seated side by side on the big white couch.

"John Barany?" She gave me a puzzled look.

"I heard he got out of the hospital a few days ago."

"Who's John Barany?"

I looked her straight in the eye. "Don't you know?"

She frowned thoughtfully. "Wait a minute. Isn't he

one of those gangsters who was shot a couple of weeks ago?"

"That's right."

"Well why on earth would he come to Jerry's funeral?"

"The police showed me some pictures of Jerry at a birthday party for Frank Tarabola. He's another one of the gangsters that got shot."

"So?"

"John Barany was in a couple of them."

"I still don't see . . ."

"In one of the pictures he was dancing with you."

"Oh." She looked away while she thought about it. "I guess we did go to some affair like that. It's hard to remember everyone you dance with."

"Gloria." She looked at me. "I saw him coming out of this building yesterday," I told her.

"Oh. Well, all right, he is an old friend. Jerry and I have known him and Marie for years. Jerry used to do odd jobs for him once in a while."

"Don't you think it's a little risky, him calling on you so soon?"

She stiffened. "What is this, Elliot? Why all these questions?" She smiled wryly. "Are you up for a part in some play about the Spanish Inquisition?"

"Let me ask just one more," I said. "Didn't you once tell me you won the Montana girl's championship for pistol shooting?"

The question took her by surprise. It was a few moments before she answered. When she did she looked directly at me.

"That was rifle shooting. In pistol I was Missoula County champion. State runner-up."

There was a long, uncomfortable silence while we stared at each other. Then she stood up.

"I'll get some more coffee," she said quietly.

"John is getting out of the rackets," she said when she returned. "He was telling me yesterday how happy he is about it. He never liked being mixed up in it, you know. Just sort of married into the mob and couldn't get out."

"I guess it's lucky for him that Frank Tarabola was killed."

"Frank Tarabola is no great loss to the world."

"No, I guess not. And Barany's also free of his wife, isn't he? That's even luckier. As soon as her body turns up, that is."

"He's a very nice man, Elliot. I wish you knew him."

"I'm sure he's a real sweetheart."

"He's as gentle as a lamb. Did you know that Barany means lamb in Hungarian?"

Her voice was soft and husky, and there was a far-away look in her eyes. It occurred to me she was in love with the guy.

"Hungarian lamb must be pretty tough," I said.

"Elliot . . ."

"No, listen to me, Gloria. Let me tell you what I've been thinking about."

She gave me a look of apprehension.

"I've been trying to figure out who killed Frank Tarabola," I said, "and wounded John Barany. The police think it was Marie Barany and so does the Tarabola mob, I guess. But I don't believe that."

Her eyes widened a bit, and she chewed nervously on her lower lip.

"Roxanne was stealing from the organization," I

continued, "and Jerry was helping her. I think that much is true. And Nero put his investigator Lemay on Roxanne's tail to find out what was going on. That gave Jerry and Marie the opportunity they'd been looking for. They hatched a plan to kill Barany and throw the blame on Roxanne."

"But—"

"Let me finish. The plan was this: Jerry made a deal with Lemay to do away with Roxanne in return for her share of the money. Then they hired an actress to impersonate her so the mob would think she was still alive. At the same time they had her hire a hit man to make it look like she was out to kill the Baron. And, of course, the guy they had play the part of the hit man would never do the job. He didn't even give a very convincing performance, I'm embarrassed to say. They probably counted on that, in fact. That way Marie could put on a blonde wig and shoot her husband right out on the street in front of witnesses, and everyone would think Roxanne had decided to do the job herself."

"But that's what happened," she insisted.

"No it isn't. That's what was supposed to happen. What Jerry didn't count on was Lemay's loyalty to his boss. Or maybe Lemay was just too timid to take a chance on crossing the mob. He reported the whole thing to Nero, who had him pretend to go along with the scheme."

"You don't know that. You're only guessing."

"Yes, but it fits, doesn't it? Nero had been chafing for a long time under Tarabola's rule, trying to change the way the mob was operating. He must have been itching for a chance to get rid of Tarabola, and Jerry's plan gave it to him. All he had to do was enlist the cooperation of Barany, who had his own reasons for wanting Tarabola out of the way. Together they laid a trail of false evidence—planting a half-burnt wig in the incinerator, taking Marie's revolver for the killer to use. Then all they had to do was carry out Jerry's plan a day in advance, the only change in the scenario being that Barany was only wounded, not too seriously, and Tarabola was killed by what looked like a stray shot."

I paused to catch my breath.

"Of course, they had to kill Lemay to keep him quiet, but that was no problem. And they could make Jerry and Marie look like victims of mob revenge. Nero must have enough henchmen to help him get rid of those two without asking any questions.

"The thing I couldn't figure out was who they got to do the actual shooting. Until I recalled seeing the picture of you dancing with Barany and remembered that you were a pistol champion back home in Montana."

She put her eyes down, averting my gaze. After a moment she raised them, her look a mixture of contrition and belligerence.

"Gloria, do you realize what you've gotten into?"

"Johnny's selling out all his interests in New York. We're going to Montana together." Her eyes took on a dreamy look. "We're going to open up a luxury resort, something to rival Vail. Skiing in the winter, sailing and fishing in the summer. And a three-star restaurant with the best Hungarian cuisine in North America."

"And Gary? What about him?"

"He and Johnny get along great. Johnny's very

good to him. He always wanted a son. Jerry hardly ever talked to Gary."

"Everything works out very handy, doesn't it?"

"Anyway," she said defiantly, "all you have is a theory. There's no way to prove it."

"Think about it," I replied. "If I've doped things out, don't you think the police will?"

"Johnny says they don't care. That FBI man has an important new job in Washington and is too busy to think about it, and the New York City police are just happy to have the case closed."

"Even Walter Baily?"

"Johnny says not to worry about him. He's retiring soon, and Johnny says everything will be taken care of."

"I wouldn't be so sure."

"Anyway, Johnny says the cops knew something fishy was going on the whole time, that they knew Roxanne was dead, but they just played along to see what would happen. Now that Tarabola's dead they have no interest in who did it. That's what Johnny says."

"Are you trying to tell me that Baily knew all the time that the woman who hired me wasn't Roxanne Adair? That it was all a set-up?"

"Johnny says he heard through the grapevine that they'd already found Roxanne's body but that Baily was keeping it quiet to see what would happen."

As I sat there trying to digest this latest information she took hold of both my hands and looked earnestly into my eyes.

"I love him, Elliot. He's very good to me."

I stared back at her and thought of the gawky

young actress I had known, fresh from Montana and out to take New York by storm.

" 'Let me not to the marriage of true minds admit impediments,' " I said.

17

"Don't get me wrong," said Phil Bender. "You're welcome to stay as long as you want."

"I appreciate that, Phil."

"And I appreciate how well you kept the place while I was gone. It really wasn't necessary to have the furniture reupholstered."

"Just my way of showing my gratitude."

"And that crack in the door of the commode is hardly noticeable. You needn't worry about it."

"I'm glad you feel that way."

He grinned. "It must have been quite a party."

"That it was," I said.

The grin gave way to a worried frown. "The only item I'm a little worried about is my Ching dynasty vase. I haven't been able to find it."

A porcelain expert had informed me it was beyond repair, but a gallery on East Eighty-seventh Street had one that might pass as a replacement. The trouble was it cost two thousand dollars.

"I stored it at my mother's house for safekeeping," I told Phil. "I'm going up there in a few weeks and I'll bring it back."

"That was very thoughtful of you," he said. "It makes me feel even worse about asking you to find somewhere else to stay tonight."

"Don't worry about it," I assured him.

"It's just that I'm having someone over for dinner, and if things work out, she may stay. So if you could possibly find somewhere else to bunk up, just for tonight . . ."

"Sure. No problem. I'm having dinner with a guy from Washington who's staying at the Hotel Wellington. I may take a room there for the night."

"The Wellington? Boy, you must have struck it rich. What have you been up to while I was gone?"

"Not much," I answered. "I almost starred in a hit."

"It's nice of you to have dinner with me," said Tony Bonello. "I don't get to New York much these days, and most of the people I know are busy with other things."

"My pleasure," I replied. "I'm grateful to you for not initiating charges against me for my stint as a con man."

"Oh, that reminds me," he said. "How's Amanda Cole?"

Now we were down to business. As I suspected, he had invited me to dine in order to pump me for information about Amanda.

"Okay, I guess. To tell you the truth, I haven't seen her in almost a month."

"I called her a few times from Washington, but she seemed, well, a little standoffish."

"I know what you mean. I think she doesn't want to commit herself to anything."

"I thought maybe you and she had some sort of understanding," Bonello said.

"I thought so myself, but I guess I was wrong. She's a funny girl."

I did not tell him that Amanda had called me that morning to give me her new address.

"Anything new with the case?" I asked.

"Not since we found Marie Barany's body. I think we're about to close it. The New York Police Department already has."

"I guess that means that Baily is satisfied."

"More or less. He's talking about retiring. All excited about some new job offer."

"Oh?"

"It won't come through till next spring, but he says it's in the bag. Going to move to Montana and become chief of security of some new luxury resort. From the way he talks I think he owns a piece of it."

"Oh."

"He's very excited. Even bought a ten-gallon hat and a string tie."

"I hope he likes paprika," I said.

"What do you mean?"

"Oh, nothing. Listen, there's something I wanted to ask you."

"What's that?"

I searched for a way to pose my question.

"I heard—er, someone told me, that is—that Baily knew all the time that Amanda was really an actress."

"Oh? Where did you hear that?"

"Just a rumor. In fact, I heard that he already knew Roxanne was dead before Amanda and I ever got into the picture."

He took a while to respond.

"There were things about that investigation I didn't approve of," he said stiffly. "It really wasn't my jurisdiction."

It was clear he was not going to say anything more about it. We ate for a while in awkward silence.

"How's your new job?" I asked. "Do you miss keeping track of Don Eraldo?"

"Not really," he answered. "Too busy. Besides, there's nothing to keep track of. The Don's retired."

"No kidding."

He nodded. "Bought a farm upstate. I think the shooting scared him. Made him realize he's too old to stay in business."

"You think he's gone for good?"

Bonello shrugged. "You never know. I'm sure he'll come down to the city from time to time. From what I hear he's maintaining an apartment in Manhattan. If I know him, the two things that will bring him to town are opera and women."

"I think you have something that belongs to me." Michael Nero leaned back in the imitation Louis XV armchair and crossed his legs.

"How on earth did you find me here?" I asked.

"I stopped by your apartment on my way to the office. Your roommate told me you had spent the night at the Wellington." He looked like a cat when he smiled. "I'm afraid he was rather upset at being disturbed so early. Please convey my apology."

"Yeah, sure."

"And I'm afraid my chauffeur behaved rather rudely in return, but I'm sure the bruise won't take long to heal."

"Your chauffeur? You mean Muzio? The thug who's standing guard outside my door?"

"That's right. I forgot you'd already met. As you

know, he has a bit of a mean streak. It's unpleasant, but useful at times."

He gave me a smug look.

"Just what is it you want from me?" I asked.

"About a month ago you took a Chrysler New Yorker from a parking lot on West Thirty-ninth Street. There was an overnight case in the trunk containing some things that belonged to me. When I got them back something was missing."

I tried to look blank.

"Fenway, don't play games with me. As you've already seen, I'm not a good sport."

"I only took two thousand dollars," I said. "It cost me almost that much to repair the damage your goons did my apartment."

"I don't know what you're talking about. I'm looking for a notebook."

"Notebook?"

"Fenway, I'm late for an appointment. Give me the notebook or I'll turn you over to Muzio and you'll never eat solid food again."

"You know, Nero, I'm sick of being threatened. That notebook you mentioned is in safe hands, and the party who has it has instructions to forward it to Agent Tony Bonello of the FBI if anything happens to me."

He grinned.

"Fenway, you're wonderful. The entertainment value is almost worth the aggravation. I never heard anyone say anything like that outside a movie. Do you really expect me to believe it?"

Stony silence, I decided, was my best response.

"Even if it were true," he went on, "we could easily get you to rescind those instructions. We could visit your parents in Cranston, for instance, and ask them to intercede with you on our behalf."

"You bastards don't stop at anything, do you?"

"Why make things unpleasant? That notebook is of no use to you."

"It's my insurance," I replied. "A guarantee that nothing will happen to me or Amanda Cole."

He laughed delightedly. "Happen to you? Why should anything happen to you? Do you think we have any interest in you, other than getting our property back?" He gave me a frank, open look. "Believe me, we have nothing to gain by doing you harm. In fact, it would only serve to reopen a case that is virtually closed."

I thought about that. What he said made sense.

"I give you my word," he said in an earnest tone, "that once the notebook is returned you have nothing to fear from us. And you can rest easy about Miss Cole." He gave me a smarmy look. "She is well protected."

"What the hell does that mean?"

"Nothing, nothing. Look, I'll make a deal with you. Give me the notebook and I'll forget about the two thousand you kept. That way you won't feel you gave it up for nothing."

The son of a bitch was so generous he could have been an agent.

"I have to replace a vase your goons broke," I said. "Ching dynasty. It costs two thousand."

"Celadon?" he asked.

"Yes," I answered.

"How tall?"

"About twelve inches."

"Sounds a little overpriced," he said. "But, of

course, it's impossible to tell without seeing it. On the whole I think Kangxi pieces are better investments."

"Throw in the two thousand for the vase," I said, "and the notebook is yours."

He smiled. "Why not? It would be demeaning to offer an assassin of your caliber anything less."

We arranged for me to bring the notebook to his law office in downtown Brooklyn that afternoon and collect the money for the vase. We even shook hands as he left.

"I underestimated you, Fenway," he told me. "You're a cool customer, cooler than I thought. And you have a hell of a lot of nerve."

I smiled briefly in acknowledgment. "In my business you have to," I said.

Amanda's new apartment was on Sutton Place, a short taxi ride from the Wellington. After my interview with Nero I went over to see it.

"I have to go out, Elliot," said Amanda. "You should have phoned first."

"I was in the neighborhood," I explained. "Wow! This is some place. It must cost a bundle."

"Everything in New York is expensive, don't you think?"

"Well . . ."

"It will look nice once it's all furnished, instead of just bare bones the way it is now."

"It looks pretty well furnished to me. Did you inherit some money?"

"I'm going shopping for a new bedroom suite this morning, as a matter of fact. A friend of mine is taking me."

"Oh. Well, I have nothing to do. Mind if I tag along?"

"It might be better if you didn't."

An awkward silence followed, broken by the sound of the doorbell.

"I guess that's my friend." Amanda looked flustered. "This is a little embarrassing."

She opened the door and there stood dapper little Vinnie, dressed, appropriately enough, in a sharkskin suit. He curled his lip at me. His teeth looked newly sharpened.

"What's he doing here?" he wanted to know.

I gaped at him. "You're going shopping with Vinnie?" I asked Amanda.

"Not exactly," she replied.

"Don Eraldo is waiting in the car," said Vinnie.

"The Don? You're going shopping with the Don?"

"I wish you had called first," she said.

"Don Eraldo does not like to be kept waiting," Vinnie informed her.

"And I don't like to be rushed," she replied in a cool voice, looking directly at him. "Please go downstairs and tell Eraldo I'll be down in a few minutes."

He glared back at her, but her look did not waver. Then he turned and bared his teeth at me. I put my hand up to my throat.

"Don't take too long," he said. "The Don won't like it."

I waited until he closed the door before speaking.

"Eraldo? You call him Eraldo?"

"It's his name," she said.

"What does he call you?"

"Violetta." She giggled. "After some character in an opera."

"It figures," I said. "She was a kept woman."

"Don't be a prig, Elliot."

"This is his apartment, isn't it? He's paying the rent."

"He's interested in promoting my career. He has an awful lot of money."

"He's a mobster. He has people killed."

"It isn't easy to make a go of it in the theatre without some help."

"He's also senile."

"He wants to produce a vehicle for me to star in. A musical comedy about the life of Lucky Luciano. I'm going to play the lady in red."

"Who the hell's the lady in red?"

"The female lead."

"I figured that much."

"I could probably talk him into giving you a part."

"As what? The corpse in concrete? No, thanks. I've seen enough gangsters to last me a lifetime."

"I was hoping we could still be friends."

"Why not? Maybe we can all play bridge together —you and me and Muzio and Vinnie."

"Eraldo only comes to New York about once a month. We could see each other in between."

"Oh, sure. Until I wind up as part of a repaving project on the Long Island Expressway."

She looked at me sadly. "I really like you, Elliot. I always thought you were cute, right from the start."

"Thanks," I said. "I'll try to keep that in mind through all those long, cold, lonely nights."

"So you're the guy who doesn't show up for dates."

Teresa's brother Angelo grinned at me as he shoved a forkful of lasagna into his mouth.

"Angelo!" Teresa's mother spoke sharply. "Elliot already explained that. He was working under cover for the FBI. You should be proud Teresa has a boyfriend who does such important work."

"Ma!" Teresa pleaded. "Elliot isn't my boyfriend. He's just a friend."

"All right, all right, so sue me." Mrs. Gianelli winked at me. "How do you like the lasagna, Elliot? Teresa can really cook, huh?"

After dinner Teresa took me to the basement where a wizened old man with a two-day growth of white beard sat in his undershirt watching television.

"*Nonno,*" she said to him, "this is my friend, Elliot. Elliot, this is my grandfather."

The old man peered at me. "Where you from?" he asked.

"Where am I from? Rhode Island, originally. But now I live in Manhattan."

"No, no." He looked irritated. "What *ragione?* What *provincia?*"

"He means what part of Italy do you come from," Teresa explained. "Elliot's not Italian, *Nonno.*"

The old man made a noise like spitting.

"What happened to that Patrizio boy you was going with? So what his father come from Abruzzo. These days you can't be choosy."

Back upstairs I had a glass of wine with the *pater famiiias* while Teresa and her mother did the dishes.

"What do you plan to do with yourself after you quit acting?" he wanted to know.

"I wasn't planning on quitting acting," I replied.

He gave no indication of having heard me as he took a long swallow of wine and then wiped his mouth with the back of his hand.

"Me and my sons, we got a good business. Scrap iron. We could use a bright guy to handle our accounts." He grinned in a friendly way. "I'm holding it open for Teresa's husband, whenever he comes along."

Teresa walked me to the bus.

"I hope my father didn't lean on you too much."

"No, no, not at all. He was very nice."

"I don't know what got into my mother, doing all that talking."

"Oh, I enjoyed it. Really. She's a lovely woman."

"Hey, Elliot, I have passes for Shea Stadium next Saturday. My Uncle Ralph works there. Mets versus the Cardinals. You want to go?"

"Gee, Teresa, I'd love to, but I have to go up to Rhode Island. It's my parents' wedding anniversary."

"Oh." She looked a bit crestfallen.

"I'll be in touch, though. Very soon."

Teresa got engaged last month to the Patrizio boy. Her grandfather must be very happy. It took a few weeks for the announcement to catch up with me. That's the way it is when you're on the road.

Tonight we're in Davenport, Iowa. It's not so bad being a Hunk. Better than I expected. The air-conditioning is sometimes a little strong and the audiences can get pretty raucous, but the pay is good and you get to see a lot of the country. All in all, I can't complain.

And it is only temporary. Morrie sent a note a couple of weeks ago to show he hasn't forgotten me. He said there is a slim chance I'll be written back into "A Brighter Tomorrow" now that Dr. Todd Duncan has left the show to do a movie. They're thinking of having me turn up with amnesia, the idea being that I was picked up by a garbage scow after my plunge into the river. Of course, it's all very iffy, but it doesn't hurt to have a little hope.

Speaking of movies, I saw the one Maud made. I thought it was dreadful, but I guess her career is launched. On the other hand, Amanda is still waiting for her big break, since *LUCKY!* folded without ever reaching New York.

I think about Amanda a lot. She was really something. I was reminded of her just the other night when I found a phone number on a slip of paper in my wallet. It took me a long time to recall what it was, but when I did it sure set off a chain of memories.

Remember when we were in room 311 of the Hotel Clayton together, when she was pretending to be Roxanne and I was pretending to be Raven? We exchanged phone numbers, remember? So we could get in touch with each other in case we had to. As soon as I realized what it was I gave the number a try.

It turned out to be a dry cleaner's on Amsterdam Avenue.

These days it's hard to keep your faith in human nature.

ABOUT THE AUTHOR

Born and raised in Brooklyn, N. J. McIver is now a
mathematics professor in the Midwest. *An Assassin
Prepares* is his first novel for the Crime Club; his first,
Come Back, Alice Smythereene!, was published by St.
Martin's Press in 1985.